THE WORLD OF
NORM
MUST BE WASHED SEPARATELY

ORCHARD BOOKS
338 Euston Road, London NW1 3BH
Orchard Books Australia
Level 17/207 Kent Street, Sydney, NSW 2000

First published in 2014 by Orchard Books

A Paperback Original

ISBN 978 1 40832 951 1

Text © Jonathan Meres 2014
Illustrations © Donough O'Malley 2014

A CIP catalogue record for this book is available from the British Library.

1 3 5 7 9 10 8 6 4 2

Printed in Great Britain

Orchard Books is a division of Hachette Children's Books,
an Hachette UK company.

www.hachette.co.uk

JONATHAN MERES

THE WORLD OF NORM

MUST BE WASHED SEPARATELY

ORCHARD

To my lovely agent, Lucy. Less 10%

CHAPTER 1

Norm knew it was going to be one of those days when he was woken by the noise of an elephant breaking wind in the next room. Or at least that's what it **sounded** like to Norm. Not that Norm had ever actually **heard** an elephant breaking wind

in the next room before
– or any other room
for that matter – but
he imagined that's
what it would sound
like if he ever did.
Then again, thought
Norm, you only had
to close a door
slightly too hard in
this stupid little house
and it sounded like the
whole flipping world

was about to end. So actually, thinking about it, thought Norm, thinking about it, it might **not** have been an elephant breaking wind after all. It could have been just about **anything**. For all Norm knew, it could've been his **dad** breaking wind. Or his mum for that matter. Maybe his mum and dad had broken wind at exactly the same time. Maybe that's what adults did when they'd been together for as long as his parents had. Their digestive systems somehow synchronised and they ended up doing just about **everything** at the same time.

Norm shuddered. What on earth was he doing, thinking about his parents' bodily functions at **this** time on a Sunday morning? Frankly, thought Norm, he had no particular wish to think about his parents' bodily functions at **any** time, let alone before he'd even got out of bed. Especially before he'd even had breakfast.

"Norm!" yelled a distant, muffled-sounding voice.

Funny, thought Norm, propping himself up on one elbow and looking around. Where was that coming from? Because there was only **one** person who ever called him **Norm**.

"Mikey?" said Norm getting out of bed. "Where are you?"

"Over here!" said the distant, muffled-sounding voice.

"Where?" said Norm getting more confused by the second.

"Here!"

"Gordon flipping Bennet!" said Norm, padding over to the window and opening the curtains. But there was no one outside. This was starting to get seriously weird. Norm was beginning to get ever so slightly freaked out. Perhaps he hadn't woken up at all. Perhaps he was still asleep and in the middle of a dream. But then, thought Norm, if he was in the middle of a **dream**, how would he actually **know** he was in the middle of a dream?

"NORM!" screamed Mikey. "I'M ON THE **PHONE!**"

"Uh? What? Where?" said Norm.

"HERE!"

Norm spun round to see his phone lying on the floor, next to the bed. What was it doing there, instead of on his bedside table? What was going on exactly? Or even roughly?

"You still there?"
said Norm
picking up the
phone and
putting it to his
ear.

"'Course I am!"
laughed Mikey.
"Where else
would I be?"

"What?"
said Norm.

"You must've
fallen back to sleep
and dropped your phone, Norm!"

Norm pulled a face. "Uh? What do you mean?"

"Well, we were talking and then you just went quiet. I didn't realise I was *that* boring!"

"Seriously?" said Norm. "We were *talking?*"

"Yeah," said Mikey. "I called you! Don't you remember?"

Norm thought for a moment. "Not really, no."

"Really?"

"Are you winding me up, Mikey?"

"Honestly, I'm not, Norm," protested Mikey. "Why would I do that?"

It was a fair point, thought Norm. If Mikey was going to make something up, he might as well make something *decent* up. Not something completely rubbish like pretending to call somebody when he actually hadn't.

"What do you reckon, by the way?" said Mikey.

"What do I reckon about *what?*" said Norm.

"Hang on a minute."

"PAAAAAAAAAARP!"

Norm stood holding his phone, more and more convinced that he really **was** in the middle of a dream. Either that or this was already shaping up to be one of the weirdest days of his life so far. And **that** was flipping saying something.

"PAAAAAAAAAARP!" went something like a foghorn on the other end of the line..

"Gordon flipping Bennet, Mikey!" yelled Norm. "You nearly blew my flipping head off!"

Mikey laughed. "It's just a trombone, Norm!"

A **trombone**? thought Norm. So that's what the sound had been. It **hadn't** been an elephant breaking wind after all! Or his mum and dad. Or anyone else, for that matter.

It was simply **Mikey** trying to wake him up after he'd dozed off to sleep again!

"I didn't know you played the trombone, Mikey."

"I don't."

"What?"

"I don't."

"But..."

"It's my mum's," said Mikey.

"Your **mum** plays the trombone?"

"Yeah."

"I never knew that," said Norm.

"There are lots of things you don't know about my mum, Norm."

"Uh?"

"She's a woman of mystery," said Mikey mysteriously.

"Really?" said Norm.

"No, not really," said Mikey.

Norm sighed. It was much too early for this. Perhaps if Mikey called back later and they repeated the entire conversation word for word, then maybe – just **maybe** – it would make **slightly** more sense. Even then, Norm wasn't convinced.

"So?" said Mikey.

"So, what?" said Norm.

"Do you want to, or not?"

Norm sighed again. "Do I want to **what**, or not?"

"Go **biking?**"

"Biking?" said Norm. "Why didn't you say so in the first flipping place?"

"I **did**," said Mikey.

"What?" said Norm.

"I **did** say so," said Mikey. "Several times actually."

"Well, I didn't hear you."

"That's because you'd fallen back to sleep!"

"Oh, right."

"So do you?""

"Are you **serious**, Mikey?" said Norm. "Do I want to go **biking?**"

"Yeah," said Mikey.

"Do I want to go biking?"

"Yeah."

"'Course I want to go flipping biking, you doughnut! What kind of stupid question is **that**?"

"What time?" said Mikey.

"What time is it now?" said Norm.

"Half past."

"Half past what?"

"Nine."

"Whoa," said Norm.

"And before you ask, it's **Sunday!**" laughed Mikey.

"I know **that!**" said

Norm. "I'll be round at your place at quarter to."

"Quarter to what?" said Mikey.

"Ten," said Norm.

"But that's only…"

"Yeah, I know," said Norm cutting his best friend off. "I'll get a move on. Don't you worry about **that!**"

"'Kay," said Mikey. "See you soon then, Norm."

"Yeah, see you," said Norm.

"Oh and Norm?"

"What?"

"You won't fall asleep **again**, will you?"

"Very funny, Mikey," said Norm ending the call and looking round for some clothes to climb into.

CHAPTER 2

Norm got dressed as fast as he could – which still wasn't all *that* fast – before bounding down the stairs with a positive spring in his step. Having his head blown off by a trombone might not have been the *best* start to the day, but the *rest* of the day was going to be pretty flipping awesome! How could it *not* be pretty flipping awesome when he was going *biking*?

To say that Norm *loved* biking would be an

understatement. As far as Norm was concerned, biking was every bit as essential as eating and sleeping and breathing. Well, eating and sleeping anyway. Even *Norm* had to admit that breathing was a *bit* more essential than biking. But only a bit.

Luckily for Norm, his best friend Mikey also loved biking, although maybe not quite as much as Norm did. Or even **nearly** as much as Norm did. Which made it doubly annoying, as far as Norm was concerned, that Mikey was naturally just that little bit **more** talented at biking than **he** was. Trebly annoying when you considered that it was Norm who dreamt of one day becoming World Mountain Biking Champion and not **Mikey**. Quadruply annoying that Mikey had a better bike! But

Norm wasn't bothered about any of that right now. All Norm wanted to do was to get a bowlful of supermarket own-brand Coco Pops down his neck as quickly as possible and ride off into the sunset. Not that the sun was anywhere near setting. It had only just risen. A bit like Norm.

"Morning, love," said Norm's mum as Norm breezed into the kitchen and plonked himself down at the table, where his brothers were already sat scoffing cereal – in Dave's case, supermarket own-brand Corn Flakes and in Brian's, supermarket own-brand Cheerios.

"Morning, Mum," chirped Norm.

"Well, **someone** sounds happy this morning!" said Norm's mum.

"Yeah, well I **am!**" said Norm.

"Really?" said Norm's mum doubtfully.

"Abso-flipping-lutely, Mum!"

"Language," said Dave spraying a mouthful of own-brand Corn Flakes all over the table.

"Creep," muttered Norm.

"Muuuum!" wailed Dave. "Norman called me a..."

"I heard," said Norm's mum.

"Don't eat with your mouth full, Dave!" said Brian.

Dave pulled a face. "What?"

"Er, I mean, don't **speak** with your mouth full," said Brian. "Obviously."

"What's it got to do with **you**, Brian?" said Dave.

"Now, now, you two," said Norm's mum. "Just eat your breakfast, there's good boys."

Norm smiled quietly to himself. Even his brothers' bickering failed to dampen his mood. If anything, it actually made Norm feel even **better**, because he knew that he wouldn't have to put up with it for much longer and that in a few short minutes he'd be burning some serious rubber, zooming through the woods, on the hill behind the precinct. It might not be **extreme** mountain-biking, but as Grandpa would say, it was better than a slap in the face with a wet fish.

"Well, love?" said Norm's mum expectantly.

"Well what?" said Norm.

"Are you going to tell us what you're so happy about?"

"Oh, you know," said Norm. "Just going biking."

Norm's mum stopped what she was doing and turned to face the table.

"Pardon?"

"I'm going biking. With Mikey."

"When?"

"Now," said Norm. "Well, as soon as I've finished breakfast, anyway."

"Oh," said Norm's mum.

"What?" said Norm, instantly sensing that something was wrong. Or at least that something was about to go wrong.

"Erm..."

"What, Mum?" said Norm, doing his best to keep calm.

"You've forgotten, haven't you, love?"

Gordon flipping Bennet! thought Norm. **What** had he flipping forgotten? He had no idea! If he **knew** what it was he might not have flipping forgotten it in the first flipping place!

"We're going to your cousins' today."

"What?" said Norm.

"For lunch."

"WHAT?" said Norm.

"And then we're going for a walk."

"WHAAAAAAAAAAAAT?" said Norm.

"You heard," said Norm's mum.

Norm **had** heard.

"I'm not going," said Norm emphatically.

"You are, love."

"You can't make me."

"I think you'll find I *can*."

"But..."

"What?" said Norm's mum.

"I'm going biking with Mikey! It's all arranged!"

"Well, I'm very sorry, Norman, but you're just going to have to *un*arrange it."

"I can't!"

"I think you'll find you *can*."

"But...but...but!" spluttered Norm. "Gordon flipping Bennet!"

"Oh, come on," said Norm's mum. "It's not the end of the world."

"I think you'll find it *is*," said Norm.

Norm's mum smiled. "There's always *next* Sunday!"

Next Sunday? thought Norm. That was like... like...a whole flipping week away or something! **Anything** could happen between now and then. Sea levels might rise due to global flipping warming or whatever and there might not actually **be** anywhere to go biking by then! Not that Norm actually **lived** anywhere near the sea. But that wasn't the point. "I'll pay you."

"Pardon?" said Norm's mum.

"I'll pay you," said Norm.

"What for?"

"If you don't make me go."

Norm's mum laughed. "Are you serious? You'd actually **pay** me?"

Norm nodded vigorously.

"You don't have any money," said Dave.

"Shut it, you!" hissed Norm.

"I'll lend you some, if you like?" said Brian.

"What?" said Norm.

"How much do you want?"

"Look, I'm sorry, love, but you're coming with us and that's all there is to it," said Norm's mum.

"But..."

"No buts, Norman. You're coming. End of."

"Well, thanks **very** much, Mum," said Norm, getting up from the table and storming out of the kitchen as dramatically as possible.

"What for?"

"FOR RUINING MY LIFE!"

"Language," said Dave.

But Norm didn't hear. He was already half way up the stairs.

CHAPTER 3

Norm threw himself down on his bed, practically oozing with anger and seething with resentment. To be told that he couldn't go biking was bad enough. But to be told that the reason he couldn't go biking was because he had to go and see his cousins? That was just about the worst thing imaginable. In fact, never mind just **about** the worst thing imaginable. It **was** the worst thing imaginable. Frankly, it was barbaric. It was inhumane. It was all Norm's worst nightmares rolled into one. As for being forced to go on a flipping **walk** with them?

That didn't even bear **thinking** about. Which was precisely why Norm was doing his best not to think about it.

Norm took a deep breath, before exhaling very slowly and **very** noisily. His cousins. His perfect flipping cousins. Danny, Becky and Ed. All of them **best** at something or other. All of them top of the **class** at something or other. All of them amazing on some stupid musical instrument Norm had never even **heard** of. All of them always out doing good deeds and baking cakes in order to raise funds for underprivileged guinea pigs or whatever. And **all** of them unbe-flipping-lievably annoying. But not nearly as annoying as the fact that their mum never, **ever** stopped banging on about them, or ever missed a single opportunity to tell anybody within earshot just how incredible her offspring were.

And when it came to Auntie Jem, 'anyone within earshot' basically meant anyone within a five mile flipping radius, because Auntie Jem had a voice like a flipping foghorn and could easily have got a job scaring birds off airport runways just by shouting at them. Not like Uncle Steve, thought Norm. Uncle Steve was the complete opposite. Not that he wasn't **proud** of his children and their almost superhuman achievements. Of course he was proud. Why **shouldn't** he be proud? It was just that Uncle Steve obviously didn't feel the need to drone on and on and flipping on about it all the time like a parrot with verbal diarrhoea.

Why, oh why, oh flipping **why** did they have to go? thought Norm, before taking another deep breath and exhaling even **more** slowly and even **more** noisily.

There was a knock at the door.

"Norman?" said Norm's dad anxiously.

"Yeah?" said Norm.

"Can I come in?"

"I dunno," muttered Norm. "**Can** you?"

"What was that?"

"Er, I said yeah, you **can** come in, Dad."

The door opened to reveal Norm's dad, still in his pyjamas and dressing gown.

"Are you, OK, son?"

"What?" said Norm.

"I heard really loud breathing. I was just making sure you were OK?"

Norm shrugged. "Depends what you mean by OK?"

"I mean not ill," said Norm's dad. "Not about to have an asthma attack. Not in need of urgent medical attention."

"Nah," said Norm. "Unfortunately."

"What?"

"Nothing," said Norm.

"So you're not ill?"

"No, I'm not ill, Dad."

"But?"

"What?" said Norm.

"There's a **but**," said Norm's dad. "I can tell."

Norm looked at his dad. There was no point saying

anything. What difference would it make? None whatso-flipping-ever.

"Come on," said Norm's dad. "Spit it out."

"Really?" said Norm uncertainly.

Norm's dad nodded. "Really."

"You really want to know?"

"I really want to know, Norman," said Norm's dad. "And preferably today."

Norm sighed again. "I don't want to go and see my cousins."

Norm's dad laughed. "You don't say!"

Norm pulled a face. "What?"

"Is that all it is? You don't want to go and see your cousins?"

"Yeah," said Norm. "I mean, no. I mean...what?"

"Well, that's not exactly earth-shattering news, is it?"

"What do you mean?" said Norm.

"Come on, son. I'm not stupid."

Norm instinctively opened his mouth to say something.

"Don't even *think* about it," said Norm's dad cutting him off before he had the chance.

Norm waited for his dad to carry on. Eventually he did.

"You think I haven't noticed?"

"Noticed what?" said Norm innocently.

"Mind if I sit down?" said Norm's dad sitting on the

end of Norm's bed anyway, before Norm could say whether or not he minded.

Gordon flipping Bennet, thought Norm. If there was one thing he couldn't stand – apart from all the other things he couldn't stand – it was having to talk to his parents about his flipping feelings and stuff. And unless Norm was very much mistaken, it looked like that was **precisely** what he was about to do. Or at least it looked like that was precisely what his dad was **expecting** him to do, anyway.

"Would you like to know a secret?" said Norm's dad, casting a nervous glance towards the door, as if he was anxious not to be overheard by anyone.

Would he like to know a **secret?** thought Norm. Exactly how old did his dad think he **was**? And besides, he already knew there was no such thing as the Tooth Fairy. Not that Norm ever found any money under his flipping pillow **these** days. Not since his dad had lost his job and they'd been forced to eat supermarket own-brand cereals and wipe their bums with supermarket own-brand flipping toilet paper he hadn't, anyway!

"Er, Dad?"

"Yeah?"

"You do know I'm nearly thirteen years old, right?"

Norm's dad smiled. "Yes, Norman. I do know that. But thanks for reminding me."

"So, what's the big 'secret', then?" said Norm making speech marks in the air with his fingers.

"Well," said Norm's dad, "you might not believe this, but..."

"What?" said Norm.

"I don't particularly want to go, either."

"Pardon?"

"I don't want to go, either."

This wasn't what Norm had been expecting at all. Not that Norm actually **knew** what he'd been expecting. But whatever it was – this wasn't it.

"You mean, to Auntie Jem's and Uncle Steve's?"

"No, I mean skateboarding in the Himalayas."

Norm sighed. He hated it when other people were sarcastic. It was OK for **him** to be sarcastic. But not for **other** people. That was **bang** out of order, that was.

"Of **course** I mean to Auntie Jem's and Uncle Steve's," said Norm's dad. "Why do you think I'm still in my pyjamas?"

Until now, Norm hadn't even **noticed** that his dad was still wearing his pyjamas. Then again, Norm wouldn't have noticed if a giant meteor had just landed in the garden.

"Surprised?"

"Er, yeah, I **am** actually, Dad."

"Thought you might be."

"Why?" said Norm.

"Why did I think you'd be **surprised?**"

"Why don't you want to go to Auntie Jem's and Uncle Steve's?"

"Ah," said Norm's dad. "That's a good question."

Yes, thought Norm. It **was** a good question. But what was the answer?

"It's been tricky ever since... ever since..."

Ever since what? thought Norm. Ever since the dawn of time? Ever since a week last Tuesday? Ever since cheese was invented?

"You really want to know, Norman?"

Norm nodded. "I really want to know."

"It's been tricky ever since..."

"What, Dad?"

Norm's dad sighed. "I haven't had a job."

38

"Oh, right," said Norm. "I see."

Suddenly Norm knew **exactly** why his dad might be reluctant to go and see Auntie Jem and Uncle Steve. He felt awkward. He somehow felt inadequate. He might even feel a bit embarrassed. Which was weird. Because Norm had never thought his dad could feel embarrassed before. He could be embarrassing. But that was another story.

"What about you, Norman?"

"What?"

"Why don't **you** want to go?"

Norm snorted. "How long have you got?"

"About an hour?"

"Uh?" said Norm. "An hour?"

Norm's dad nodded. "Before we have to leave."

"Right," said Norm.

"Go on, then."

Norm hesitated as he tried to gather his thoughts. How did he even **begin** to explain why he didn't want to go and see his perfect flipping cousins? What exactly **was** it about them that he couldn't stand? Apart from everything?

"They're just so..."

"What?"

"Just so..."

"**What**, Norman?"

Norm sighed. "Flipping annoying."

"Hmmm," said Norm's dad.

"And Auntie Jem never stops flipping going **on** about them!" said Norm.

"Yes," said Norm's dad. "I know what you mean."

Norm looked surprised. "You do?"

"I do, Norman, yes. And not only that, I know how you feel."

If Norm was surprised before, he was completely and utterly gobsmacked now.

"You **do?**"

"I do," said Norm's dad. "Would you like to know how?"

Norm nodded.

"OK," said Norm's dad. "Well, I try not to start **too** may sentences with, 'When I was **your** age,' but..."

"You're just about to?" said Norm.

"Yep. 'Fraid so."

Norm waited for his dad to go on. And on. And on and on and on.

"When I was **your** age, Norman, **my** mum and

dad had these friends…"

Gordon flipping Bennet, thought
Norm. This wasn't looking too
promising. Only five seconds
or so into the story and
already he felt like
chewing his flipping feet
off. It could only get better.
Couldn't it?

"…And **they** had a son, called…actually, it doesn't
matter what he was called."

No, thought Norm. It flipping doesn't.

"Anyway," said Norm's dad, "for **some** reason, my
parents thought it would be a really brilliant idea if
this kid and me became friends."

"And **you** didn't think it was a good idea?"

"Correct," said Norm's dad.

"Why?"

"Why?"

Norm nodded.

"Because he was **unbelievably** annoying, Norman. That's why."

"Right," said Norm.

"The thing was," said Norm's dad, "**his** mum and dad wouldn't hear a bad word said against him. As far as **they** were concerned the sun shone out of his..."

Norm's dad suddenly stopped. Wherever it was that the sun shone out of, he clearly wasn't about to say. Besides, Norm had a pretty good idea where it was anyway. Not only that but he was beginning to see **why** his dad was telling him all this.

"So, what was so annoying about him, Dad?"

"Ha!" said Norm's dad. "What **wasn't** annoying about him, more like?"

"OK," said Norm. "What **wasn't** annoying about him, then?"

"Nothing!" said Norm's dad. "There was **nothing** that wasn't annoying about him!"

Norm couldn't help smiling. His dad really **did** know how he felt!

"ARE YOU TWO READY YET?" called Norm's mum from the foot of the stairs.

"IN A MINUTE!" called Norm and his dad together, before looking at each other and bursting out laughing.

CHAPTER 4

Norm was actually the first one out of the house. Which was pretty weird, considering he'd sooner have his teeth pulled out one by one with a pair of rusty pliers – **without** anaesthetic – than go and see his perfect flipping cousins. But deep down, Norm **knew** that he really didn't have much choice. Well, he could **try** hatching up some hare-brained plan and avoid going to see them by pretending to be dead, or emigrating to Belgium or something. But he knew resistance was futile. And anyway, even if he **did** choose not to go and his parents actually **allowed** him to stay behind, he'd end up paying for it till he was thirty and possibly even older. So he knew that he might as well just grin and bear it and get it over with. It was going to be 100% pure torture at the time, but it would be a lot less hassle in the long run.

Determined to make the most of his last few moments of freedom, Norm decided to get his bike out of the garage and do some wheelies. At least that way he could **try** to chill out just a little bit and take his mind off the inevitable horrors to come. It was certainly better than hanging about **inside** the house, waiting for his dad to get dressed and listening to his brothers squabbling like squirrels.

Norm suddenly remembered what his dad had told him. Not that it had been long since he'd told him it. It had only been a few minutes. That wasn't the point. The point was that Norm's dad had told Norm that he knew how he *felt* – and *that* hardly ever flipping happened. In fact, thought Norm, he was reasonably sure it had *never* flipping happened before. Or at least if it *had* he couldn't *remember* it happening. Then again, Norm couldn't remember which side of bed to get out of most days. But that wasn't the point, either. The point was that, as far as moments went, it had been a pretty *special* moment. So special in fact that if it had been a movie, there'd have probably been soppy music playing in the background.

"Hello, *Norman!*" said a horribly familiar sounding voice.

Norm didn't need to turn round to know that the voice belonged to Chelsea, his occasional next door neighbour. So he didn't bother.

"What flipping kept you?"

"What was that?"

Norm sighed. "Nothing."

"What are you doing, **Norman?**"

Gordon flipping Bennet, thought Norm. It was bad enough that Chelsea had a habit of popping up  like a flipping pig-tailed Jack-in-the-box whenever he was out on the drive. It was even worse that she had a habit of overemphasising his name as if it was the funniest thing she'd **ever** flipping heard. But why oh why oh flipping **why** did she always have to ask such stupid flipping questions? What was he **doing**? What did it flipping **look** like he was doing? Playing ping pong?

"Well?" said Chelsea.

"Practising wheelies," mumbled Norm.

"Why?" said Chelsea.

Norm shrugged. "Just am."

"'Just am' is **not** a proper reason, **Norman**. What are you? Six or something?"

Norm exhaled noisily.

"What's the matter?" said Chelsea. "You got a leak?"

"What?" said Norm.

"You're huffing and puffing like the Big Bad Wolf, **Norman**. Hope you're not thinking of blowing your house down?"

"I dunno what you're talking about," said Norm.

"Where's your coat, love?" said Norm's mum, emerging from the front door.

"I'm not wearing one," said Norm.

"I can see **that!**" said Norm's mum. "But where is it?"

Norm pulled a face. "Hanging up."

"Where?"

"In the hall."

"Go and get it, then."

"What?"

"Go and get your *coat*," said Norm's mum slowly and deliberately as if she was talking to a toddler.

"But I just said," said Norm, "I'm not *taking* a coat."

"Don't be ridiculous, love. Of *course* you're taking a coat! We're going for a walk with your cousins, remember?

Norm looked at his mum. Was she actually serious? Had he *remembered* he was going for a walk with his perfect flipping cousins? How could he flipping forget? That would be like forgetting to go to the flipping toilet! Except that going to the toilet was actually *fun* compared to going for a walk with his cousins. Then again, pretty much *anything* was fun compared to going for a walk with his cousins. Doing long division in Swedish whilst crawling over broken glass on his hands and knees would be fun compared to going for a walk with his **cousins**.

"Well?" said Norm's mum. "What are you waiting for?"

"But..."

"No buts, love," said Norm's mum. "Go and get your coat. Now!"

Muttering something inaudible under his breath, Norm trudged towards the front door in a right old strop, before re-emerging a few seconds later carrying his coat.

Chelsea couldn't help giggling.

"Oh hello, Chelsea," said Norm's mum turning around. "I didn't see you there."

"Hi," said Chelsea sweetly.

"That's a bit embarrassing."

"What is?"

"You hearing all that."

"Oh, that's OK," said Chelsea. "I didn't mean to laugh. Sorry."

"Doesn't matter," said Norm's mum.

Flipping typical, thought Norm. If his mum was giving Brian or Dave a telling off and **he** laughed, he'd never hear the flipping end of it! It was always the flipping same. One rule for Norm – and another rule for everybody else!

"Where are you going for a walk?" asked Chelsea.

"None of your business," said Norm.

"I was only asking."

"Yeah, well **don't!**"

"Norman!" said Norm's mum sternly.

"What?" said Norm.

"That's very rude. It was a perfectly innocent question!"

No, it flipping wasn't, thought Norm. It was anything **but** a perfectly innocent question. In fact, knowing Chelsea, it was a question specifically designed to suck up to his mum and get on his flipping nerves.

"Say sorry to Chelsea."

"WHAT?" said Norm as if his mum had just told him to run round the block in his pants.

"Say sorry."

"Seriously?" said Norm.

"Seriously," said Norm's mum.

Chelsea smiled sweetly. "Honestly, it's fine."

"It's not fine, Chelsea," said Norm's mum. "It's not fine at all."

"What seems to be the problem?" said Norm's dad appearing at the front door.

"Norman's just been very rude to Chelsea," said Norm's mum.

"Hmm," said Norm's dad. "Has he now?"

Norm's mum waited expectantly.

"Well?" she said at last. "Aren't you going to say something?"

"What?" said Norm's dad. "Oh right, erm...sorry, Chelsea."

Norm's mum pulled a face. "I mean aren't you going to say something to **Norman?**"

"Oh, I see," said Norm's dad. "Say sorry, Norman. Or...or..."

"Or **what?**" said Norm's mum, echoing Norm's own thoughts.

"I'll think of something," said Norm's dad.

"Well?" said Norm's mum glaring at Norm.

Norm sighed. "Sorry."

"That's all right," said Chelsea.

"See?" said Norm's mum. "That wasn't **so** difficult, was it?"

Norm looked at his mum. She had no idea just **how** difficult that had been. No idea at all. But before he could say anything, John the dog suddenly shot out of the door like a dribbling, hairy rocket, closely followed by Brian and Dave, both wearing their coats.

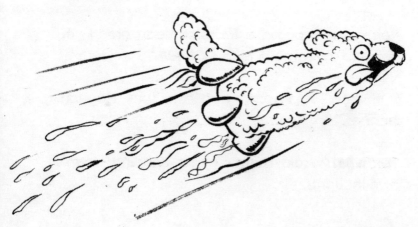

"Right, everybody," said Norm's dad. "In you get."

"Can I bring my bike, Dad?" asked Norm.

"Erm, well..." began Norm's dad.

"No, you can **not** bring your bike!" said Norm's mum before his dad had the chance to answer for himself.

"But..."

"No buts!" said Norm's mum opening the passenger door of the car and getting in. "You can't bring your bike and that's all there is to it!"

Dave laughed as he got into the back of the car.

"What is it?" said Brian, getting in beside him.

"Mum said 'buts'."

Brian shook his head. "That's **SO** immature."

"Yeah, I know," said Dave. "It's still funny, though."

Norm looked pleadingly at his dad. What about their special moment? They both knew that neither of them wanted to go and see Auntie Jem and Uncle Steve. So maybe his dad would overrule his mum and let him take his bike after all. Anything to make the experience just a little bit less painful.

"Sorry, son," said Norm's dad. "In you get."

Gordon flipping Bennet, thought Norm, getting into the car to find himself wedged between a smelly dog on one side and an even smellier **brother** on the other. So much for **that** flipping theory!

CHAPTER 5

Norm stared out the window, gradually getting more and more morose and resentful as the houses they drove past gradually got bigger and bigger and bigger. To Norm, it was yet another painful reminder that **he** used to live in a bigger house. OK, so it hadn't been as big as some of these places. Or, in fact, anything **like** as big as some of these places. But it had been bigger than the glorified shoebox they lived in now, **that** was for flipping sure. Not that it was all about the size of the house you lived in blah, blah, blah. Even Norm knew that. But well, sometimes you just didn't need any more painful reminders of how things used to be and how rubbish they were now. And **this** was most definitely one of those sometimes.

Norm's perfect cousins lived on the other side of town. But that was still **way** too close, as far as Norm was concerned. Then again, as far as Norm was concerned, his perfect cousins could live on the other side of the flipping solar system and they'd **still** be way too close. And frankly, for all they had in common with each other, they might as **well** live on the other side of the solar system. On the plus side, though, living **relatively** near to Auntie Jem's and Uncle Steve's at least meant not being stuck in the car for too long. And that was most definitely a **good** thing, because what with the combined whiff of Norm's brothers and the dog, he was beginning to have difficulty breathing.

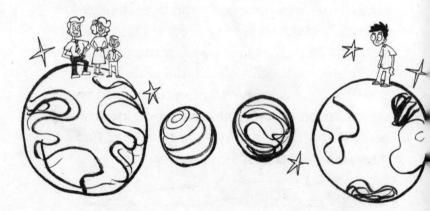

"Best behaviour now, boys," said Norm's mum as the car turned into a wide, tree lined street, with even **bigger** houses on either side.

"'Kay, Mum!" sang Brian and Dave in unison.

"Creeps," muttered Norm under his breath.

"Muuuuuuum!"
wailed Dave.
"Norman
called me
a creep!"

"No, I didn't,"
said Norm
irritably. "I called
you **and** Brian a creep."

"Pack it in, back there!" said Norm's dad, slowing down and pulling up alongside the kerb.

"Anyway, it's **creeps**," said Brian.

"What?" said Norm.

"It's creeps. Plural," said Brian. "You can't call me and Dave a **creep**. There are two of us. We're **creeps**."

"Shut up, Brian, you little freak!" hissed Norm.

"Make your mind up," said Brian.

"What?" said Norm.

"Well am I a creep, or a freak?"

"Both," muttered Norm.

"Muuuuu..." began Dave.

"I said pack it in!" said Norm's dad, the vein on the side of his head beginning to throb – a sure fire sign that he was starting to get stressed. Not that Norm noticed.

"Why do we have to be on our best behaviour, Mum?"

"What do you mean, love?" said Norm's mum.

"I mean, why do we have to be on our best behaviour?" said Norm. "Just because we're going to see our perf... Just because we're going to see *them?*"

"Because..."

"What?" said Norm.

"You just do," said Norm's mum.

Great, thought Norm. That clears *that* up, then.

"Everybody out," said Norm's dad, unbuckling his seat belt and opening his door.

Everybody did as they were told and got out of the car before setting off up the drive. Everybody, that is, except for Norm.

"You, too," said Norm's dad.

Norm sighed. "Do I **have** to, Dad?"

"I thought we'd had this conversation, Norman."

"We did, Dad."

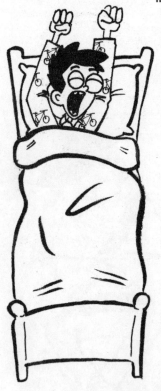

"Well, then?" said Norm's dad. "What are you waiting for?"

"To wake up," said Norm, still hoping against all odds that the whole day had somehow been one big dream.

Norm's dad smiled. "Come on. Out you get. It might not be as bad as you think it's going to be."

Norm sighed and got out of the car.

"Hi," said a voice.

"Whoa!" said Norm wheeling round and coming face to face with Danny, youngest of his three perfect cousins – and the one closest in age to him.

"Hi, Danny," said Norm's dad, heading after the others.

"Hi." Danny grinned before turning back to Norm. "So what might not be as bad as you think it's going to be?"

"What?" said Norm.

"Your dad was saying that something might not be as bad as you think it's going to be."

"Was he?" said Norm, stalling for time whilst he desperately tried to think of something. "Oh yes, that's right. He was."

"Well? said Danny. "What is it?"

"Maths," said Norm.

"Maths?"

Norm nodded.

"You were talking about **maths?** On a Sunday morning?"

Norm nodded again.

"Cool," said Danny. "Anything I can help you with?"

"What?" said Norm.

"I got the highest mark in my year for maths," said Danny.

"What do you want? A medal?" mumbled Norm.

Danny smiled. "No thanks. I've got plenty of medals already."

"Right," said Norm.

"Why didn't your dad park up the drive, by the way?" said Danny. "Your car's not *that* rubbish."

Norm thought for a moment. Knowing how his dad felt, that was probably *exactly* why he hadn't parked up the drive. Their car really *was* rubbish. His dad was *embarrassed* by it.

"Probably a good job, though," said Danny. "Be a shame to scratch our brand *new* car."

Gordon flipping Bennet, thought Norm. This surely had to be some kind of record. They'd only just arrived and already he wanted to scream. It didn't exactly bode very well for the *rest* of the day. But before Norm could get *too* worked up, a phone rang. And it wasn't *his*.

"He-llo," said Danny, whipping out a particularly snazzy looking phone and answering in one smooth movement. Norm didn't even need to ask whether it was the very latest model. That went without flipping saying. In fact, knowing his perfect cousins, it would probably be some prototype of a phone that wasn't even on sale to the general flipping public yet..

"Hi, Mum," said Danny, eyeballing Norm. "Yeah, we'll be with you in a couple of minutes."

Norm was doing his level best to remain calm in the face of considerable provocation. But it was getting increasingly difficult. It was almost as if Danny was taunting him and making a point of reminding him that his house was so big, it was quicker to **phone** each other instead of actually going to **look** for each other. And he wasn't finished there, either.

"What's that, Mum? Becky wants us to hurry up because her prize-winning Thai carrot and lemongrass soup is getting cold? We're on our way!"

"Mmmm. Hold me back," muttered Norm.

"What was that?" said Danny, putting his phone away and setting off up the drive.

But Norm wasn't even listening any more. All he could think of was how the heck he was **ever** going to survive the next few hours without going stark raving mad? How was he going to stop himself from saying something that he shouldn't? And what the **heck** was flipping lemongrass when it was at home?

CHAPTER 6

By the time Norm and Danny eventually got to the house, everyone else had already sat down for an early lunch.

"Hello, Norman," said Auntie Jem. "Glad you could join us."

"That's OK," said Norm, unsure whether Auntie Jem was being sarcastic or not. And if she **was**, how come she was only being sarcastic to **him** and not Danny as well?

"Have you washed your hands, love?" said Norm's mum.

"Yeah," said Norm.

"I think your mother means have you washed your hands **recently?**" said Auntie Jem. "Not have you **ever** washed your hands?"

"What?" said Norm.

"It's fine, Norman," said Uncle Steve. "Tuck in before it gets cold."

"Thanks," said Norm sitting down and wondering why Auntie Jem couldn't be a bit more like Uncle Steve. In other words, nice. It wasn't very long before Auntie Jem started fishing for compliments. It never was.

"Well, boys? What do you think of the soup?"

"**Super!**" Dave grinned.

Brian laughed. "Super! That's a good one, Dave!"

"Yeah, I know," said Dave. "That's why I said it!"

"Brian?"

"Yes, Auntie Jem?" said Brian.

"Are **you** enjoying the soup, as well?"

"Oh yes, it's delicious thank you, Auntie Jem!" said Brian.

"That's good, then," said Auntie Jem. "And by the way, don't thank **me**, thank Becky! **She's** the one who made it!"

"Stop it, Mummy," laughed Becky. "You're making me blush!"

Norm glanced across the dining room table. It didn't look much like his cousin was blushing to **him**. Quite the opposite, in fact, thought Norm. It looked like she was abso-flipping-lutely **loving** being the centre of attention. Just like all his perfect flipping cousins did.

"I see you're wearing your jumper, by the way, Brian," said Auntie Jem. "The one that Becky designed and knitted specially for you, using locally sourced wool."

"Mum, please!" said Becky, clearly lapping up the praise.

"It's my favourite jumper *ever,* Auntie Jem!" said Brian.

Gordon flipping Bennet, thought Norm. What did Brian have to go and say *that* for? As if Auntie Jem needed any *more* excuses to bang on about how amazing his flipping cousins were! He was *such* a flipping creep!

"It's my precious!" said Brian in a funny croaky voice.

Everyone laughed. Everyone, that is, except for Norm. Norm couldn't see what was so funny. But then Norm couldn't see what was so special about the jumper either.

Just because it had that little slimy guy from *Lord of the Rings* on it! Brian was **such** a nerd! As well as a flipping creep. Norm wouldn't have worn it if he'd been **paid** to wear it. And that was saying something because Norm would do pretty much **anything** where money was concerned. But not **that**. No flipping **way**. In Norm's opinion, the jumper wasn't merely **uncool** it was practically roasting He just didn't understand what the appeal of all that hobbity, gobliny stuff was. Then again, Norm didn't understand what the appeal of **Brian** was either, but his parents seemed to like him.

"What about you, Norman?" asked Auntie Jem.

"What?" said Norm.

"Not **what**, love!" said Norm's mum quickly. "Pardon!"

"What?" said Norm. "I mean, pardon?"

Brian and Dave giggled.

"Shut up, you little freaks!" hissed Norm through gritted teeth.

"What do *you* think of the soup?" said Auntie Jem.

"Oh, right," said Norm examining the contents of his bowl. "It's got…"

"What?" said Auntie Jem.

"Stuff floating in it," said Norm.

Auntie Jem smiled a tight-lipped smile. "Stuff?"

Norm nodded. "Sticks."

"That's the lemongrass!" laughed Danny.

Norm pulled a face. "Uh?"

"Lemongrass, love," said Norm's mum. "You know what that is! We have it all the time!"

"No, we don't," said Norm.

"I can't **believe** you didn't know that!" said Danny.

"Hey, Danny?" said Ed, Norm's eldest perfect cousin.

"Yeah?" said Danny.

"That's like, totally not cool?"

"What isn't?"

"Like, totally dissing someone for not knowing something?" said Ed. "That's like, just not cool? You know?"

Norm couldn't decide what was more annoying. Being 'like, totally dissed' for not knowing something

– whatever **that** was supposed to mean – or Ed's habit of going up at the end of every sentence as if he was asking a question?

"Ed's right, you know, Dan," said Uncle Steve. "That's not cool at all. Say sorry to Norman."

"Sorry to Norman," said Danny.

Norm shrugged. "Whatever."

"But you **do** like it, don't you?" said Auntie Jem, fixing Norm with a steely stare.

"The soup?" said Norm uncertainly.

"Yes. The soup," said Auntie Jem.

"Erm..."

"Norman's not really a big **fan** of soup," said Norm's mum.

"Really?" said Auntie Jem in a tone which suggested she'd never heard anything so ludicrous before in all her life. "But this isn't just **any** old soup. This is **prize**-winning soup!"

Norm desperately tried to think of **something** to say. **Without** creating a big stink. Which was ironic really, because in Norm's honest opinion, that was **precisely** what Becky's so-called **prize**-winning soup was doing. Creating a big stink. But he knew he couldn't say that. Or that frankly he'd seen more appetising looking bath water. As for **prize**-winning? How could you win a flipping **prize**, just for making soup? That would be like winning a prize for opening a door, or scratching your bum. Making soup wasn't a big deal. It was just

Annual Bum Scratching Competition

something you *did*. Well, something other people did, anyway.

"Well, Norman?" said Auntie Jem.

"No pressure," grinned Danny.

The room had gone very quiet. Norm suddenly felt like he was in the spotlight and that everyone was looking at him, waiting for him to deliver his verdict.

But at that moment, a phone rang. Unlike on the previous occasion, however, this time it was *Norm's* phone.

"What do you think you're *doing*, Norman?" said Norm's dad, as Norm instinctively began fishing around in his pocket.

"Answering the phone," said Norm as matter-of-factly as possible, when actually he felt like punching the air in sheer relief because it looked like he'd just been spared having to pass comment on the soup.

"Not at the **table** you're not," said Norm's dad – the vein on the side of his head beginning to throb again.

"I knew it wasn't one of **ours**," said Auntie Jem looking pointedly at Norm's mum and smiling her thin-lipped smile again. "We don't actually **allow** phones at the table. Or any other kind of electrical devices, for that matter."

They flipping **wouldn't**, would they? thought Norm bitterly. And what was so wrong about having electronic devices at the table, anyway? It was fair enough having to switch phones off and stuff when you were on a plane in case it made the plane **crash** or something. That actually made **sense** to

Norm. But banning them whilst you were eating? What was the worst that could happen? A flipping microwave malfunction or something?

By now the phone had stopped ringing and had gone to voicemail. Norm tried to have a sneaky look under the table and see who the call had been from. But clearly not quite sneakily enough.

"Norman!" hissed Norm's mum.

"What?" said Norm. "I'm just..."

"What?"

"Checking my trousers."

Brian and Dave giggled.

"Pardon?" said Norm's mum as if she couldn't quite believe what she'd just heard.

Norm sighed. **_He_** couldn't quite believe what he'd just said. And anyway he didn't need to actually look at his phone to know who the call was from. It would have been Mikey, wondering where the heck Norm had got to. What with everything else going on, Norm had completely forgotten to let his best friend know that he wouldn't be able to go biking that day after all. He'd have gone bonkers if it had been the other way round and Mikey had forgotten to tell **him**. Not that that would have happened. Mikey would never have forgotten to tell him. He'd have made sure that Norm knew as soon as possible. And anyway, Mikey never ever went bonkers about **anything**. In fact, never mind going bonkers, Mikey hardly ever got mildly miffed about anything, or even slightly cheesed off. Because Mikey was one of the nicest, most placid, level-headed people you could ever hope to flipping meet. It was **SO** flipping annoying.

"Xbox?" said Danny.

At first Norm thought he must have misheard. Surely his perfect cousins had **better** things to do than merely playing on an Xbox? Well – not

better things to do. In Norm's opinion, there were very few things actually better to do than playing on an Xbox. Biking and eating pizza immediately sprang to mind. Not at the same time, obviously. Though frankly, thought Norm, if he **could** he flipping **would**. But surely his perfect cousins had **other** things to do, rather than playing on an Xbox? Like knitting balaclavas for old people, or saving the world or something?

"Did you just say...?"

Danny nodded. "Xbox? Yeah. Why?"

"Nothing," said Norm. "Just wondered."

"Well?" said Danny. "You up for it, or not?"

For once Norm didn't even have to think for a **nanosecond**, let alone a **moment**.

"Yeah, all right, then."

"Cool," said Danny. "Once we've finished our soup."

Gordon flipping Bennet, thought Norm. He just **knew** there'd be a catch. There always flipping **was**.

"And washed up and dried and put away the dishes," said Auntie Jem, smiling her thin-lipped smile.

"Obviously, Mum," said Danny.

Yeah, right, thought Norm. **Obviously**.

CHAPTER 7

It soon became abundantly clear precisely **why** Danny seemed so keen for Norm to play on the Xbox with him. He just wanted to show off. Not only had the cousins' basement 'den' been completely pimped up to include the very latest state-of-the-art consoles, but there was also a pool table, a drum kit and the biggest screen Norm had ever seen, apart from in an actual cinema. Norm desperately tried not to seem **too** impressed or jealous. Partly because that just wouldn't have been cool – but **mainly** because he knew that Danny was **expecting** him to be impressed and jealous. He was certainly **hoping** he'd be impressed and jealous, anyway. And even if, deep down, Norm actually **was** impressed and jealous, there was no flipping **way** he was going to show it and give Danny the satisfaction of **knowing** he was. It wasn't easy, though. Especially when Norm thought about the stupid little house **he** was forced to live in. **They** didn't have a flipping den. And even if they **did**, what would they put **in** it, apart from their antique steam-driven Xbox? Never mind state-of-the-art. Theirs was more like state-of-the-flipping-**ark**!

Norm sighed.

"What's up?" said Danny.

Norm shrugged. "Nothing much."

Danny grinned. "Sure?"

Norm nodded. "Sure."

"Cool," said Danny. "So what do you fancy playing, then?"

Norm shrugged again. "Dunno. What have you got?"

"Hmm, let me see now," said Danny, before whipping out a game from behind his back with a dramatic flourish, like a magician producing a rabbit from a top hat. "How about *this?*"

Norm stared open-mouthed.

"Is that...?" he barely managed to croak.

"The brand new *Call Of Mortal Combat*?" said Danny. "As a matter of fact, yes it is."

"But..."

"But, what?" said Danny. "It only came out at

midnight last night? Yeah, I know."

Norm continued to stare at the game in his cousin's hand, like a sea lion staring at a fish. So much for not being impressed or jealous, then. It was unbe-flipping-lievable! How come Danny was allowed to play a game like this and he wasn't? His parents wouldn't let him play *Call Of flipping Mortal* **Wombat** – let alone *Call Of flipping Mortal Combat*! And he and Danny were the same age! It just wasn't flipping fair. It just wasn't flipping fair at all!

"How come...?"

"What?" said Danny. "How come I've got it when it only came out at midnight?"

Norm thought for a moment. That wasn't what he was going to ask. But now Danny came to mention it...

"Dad queued up at Games-R-Us."

"What?" said Norm. "Seriously?"

"Seriously," said Danny. "Actually he was *first* in the queue.

Naturally, thought Norm.

"It was a treat."

"What?" said Norm.

"It was a treat," said Danny. "For raising the most money."

Norm knew that he was expected to ask. So he might as well just get it over with and then they could start playing the game.

"What for?"

"Sponsored silence."

Gordon flipping Bennet, thought Norm. Sponsored silence? What a load of old nonsense **that** was. It made about as much sense as a prize for making flipping **soup**! Having said that, if he had a bit of loose change on him, right now he'd **happily** sponsor Danny to shut up for the next couple of hours.

"In aid of destitute donkeys, in case you're wondering."

Norm hadn't been wondering. Not that he had the faintest idea what a destitute donkey actually was, anyway, or how it differed from a standard donkey. And anyway, he still couldn't quite believe that Uncle Steve had actually queued up at

Please give generously

midnight to buy *Call Of Mortal Combat.* His dad wouldn't queue up for a pint of **milk** in the middle of the flipping day if his life **depended** on it, let alone for possibly the coolest game in the whole flipping universe! Norm literally couldn't **wait** to play it.

"Mum's not to know, by the way," said Danny lowering his voice and glancing anxiously towards the door.

"What?" said Norm. "You mean about the donkeys?"

"No," said Danny. "About the game."

"What?" said Norm.

"Mum's not to know about me playing *Call Of Mortal Combat.*"

"Oh."

"She wouldn't approve."

"Right."

"One of the downsides of being 'the baby' of the family, I suppose," said Danny making speech marks in the air.

Norm snorted.

"What is it?" said Danny.

"Not much fun being the **oldest**, either."

"Not that it's a competition," said Danny.

"No, course not," said Norm.

"But if it was, I'd win," grinned Danny.

Norm looked at his cousin for a moment. Did he **really** have to be quite such a flipping doughnut **all** his life? Surely he could afford to take a day off now and then? Nevertheless this was pretty interesting news.

Actually, thought Norm, this was **very** interesting news. Even Danny – his perfect cousin, Danny – did stuff without his parents' knowledge. Well, without his **mum's** knowledge, anyway. But there **were** actually chinks in his armour – or whatever that expression was. And thinking about it, thought Norm, thinking about it, there was that time he found out that Danny had faked his own school report so that he got straight As. Mind you, all **that** meant was changing one flipping B to an A. All the rest had been flipping As in the first flipping place!

"Danny?" called a muffled voice.

"Yes, Dad?" called Danny.

"You down there?"

What kind of stupid question was that? wondered Norm. Of **course** Danny was down here! What did

his dad think he was? A flipping ventriloquist or something?

"Yes, Dad, we're down here!"

"We're off! You guys need to get yourselves up here right now!"

"Coming, Dad!" said Danny immediately heading for the door.

"Off?" said Norm. "Where to?"

"For a walk," said Danny.

"But..."

"What?"

"We haven't even **played** yet!"

"Hey, that's showbiz," said Danny.

Uh? What? thought Norm. What was he on about?

94

What was showbiz? It was so flipping frustrating! If they'd come down here straight after lunch instead of having to wash and dry and put away all the flipping dishes, he might have had a chance to actually **play** *Call Of Mortal Combat* – not just look at the flipping box it came in!

"You won't say anything, will you, Norman?"

"Uh?"

"You won't say anything?" said Danny. "To my mum, I mean?"

"About what?"

"About me playing *Call Of Mortal Combat*," said Danny uncertainly. "Please?"

Norm shrugged. "Depends."

"On what?"

Norm thought for a moment. Actually, that was a very good question. What *did* it depend on? Apart from thinking of possible ways in which information like that could be used to his advantage, of course. Actually, come to think of it, thought Norm, that was it. **That** was what it all depended on. It all depended on whether he could blackmail Danny or not. That was what it all boiled down to at the end of the day. Or any time of the day, for that matter. That and how annoying Danny was going to be on the flipping walk.

"Well?" said Danny.

Norm shrugged again. "Just depends."

Danny looked at Norm for a moment before heading for the stairs.

"Let's go."

"Whatever," said Norm reluctantly following after him.

CHAPTER 8

They'd set off on the walk in one big group but it didn't take long to split up into several smaller ones. It took even less time for it to start raining. This came as no surprise to Norm, of course. But then, as far as **Norm** was concerned, the earth beneath his feet could have literally opened up and swallowed him whole – and he *still* wouldn't have been all that surprised. It wasn't as if the day could actually get much worse. He was going for a flipping *walk*! Not only that, he was going for a flipping walk with his perfect flipping **cousins**. Compared to *that*, being swallowed by the earth would come as something of a relief.

"Bet you're glad I made you bring your coat **now**, aren't you, love?" said Norm's mum.

"What?" said Norm gloomily.

"Well, if I hadn't insisted you bring it you'd have been soaked to the skin already!"

True, thought Norm. But then again, on the plus side, at least he might have caught pneumonia and been bedridden for the next few months. Which would have been a perfect excuse for staying at home the **next** time his parents suggested doing something this stupid. What was that expression? wondered Norm. Every flipping cloud has a flipping silver lining.

Norm's mum sighed. "You're not going to be like this all day, are you, Norman?"

"Like **what?**" said Norm.

"**This**," said Norm's mum. "All moody and fed up."

Norm thought for a moment. **Was** he going to be like this all day? Probably, yes. Unless, of course, the walk unexpectedly got called off. But there was more chance of **Christmas** being called off than there was of **that** happening now. It could have been raining for the previous forty days and forty nights and the flipping walk **still** wouldn't have been called off. They'd have just worn wellies and taken flipping umbrellas.

Norm could hear excited yapping ahead. It was hard to tell whether it was the dog or his brothers. Not that it mattered. And not that Norm could care less, anyway. All that Norm cared about was getting this over as quickly as possible and then locking himself in his bedroom and watching biking videos on his iPad. Not that he actually **had** a lock on his bedroom door. That wasn't the point. The point was that if he couldn't go biking with Mikey then he just wanted to be alone and do whatever he **wanted** to do. Not what his mum and dad wanted him to do.

Norm suddenly remembered the last time they'd visited his cousins. The time John had crashed into Auntie Jem and Auntie Jem had knocked the vase over and it had smashed to smithereens. Auntie Jem had gone completely ballistic and had started banging on about the vase being dead rare and coming all the way from Africa and stuff, even though Norm had a pretty good idea it had come all the way from IKEA. Either way, thought Norm, it was pretty flipping funny.

"What is it?" said Norm's mum.

"Uh?" said Norm.

"You're **almost** smiling."

Norm shrugged. "Nothing. I've just remembered something, that's all."

"Care to share?" said Norm's mum.

"Not really," said Norm, suddenly aware that Auntie Jem was approaching.

"So, Norman?" said Auntie Jem.

"Yeah?" said Norm.

"Not **yeah**," said Norm's mum. "Yes."

"Yes?" said Norm.

"What have you been up to?"

"What?" said Norm.

"Not **what?**" said Norm's mum. "**Pardon!**"

"What?" said Norm. "I mean, pardon?"

"What have you been **doing?**" said Auntie Jem. "Since I last saw you?"

Norm thought for a moment. "Washing up?"

"Mmmm, yes," said Auntie Jem. "But apart from that?"

Norm thought for another moment. "Nothing much."

"Now, now, Norman," laughed Auntie Jem. "I don't believe **that** for a single second!"

Norm wasn't particularly fussed whether Auntie Jem **believed** him or not. And besides, he knew she was only asking so that she could start banging on about his flipping cousins and bragging about everything **they'd** been up to. Not that she ever needed much of an excuse to do **that**!

"What about your biking, love?" said Norm's mum.

"Erm, well..." began Norm.

"Oh, that reminds me," said Auntie Jem, cutting

Norm off. "Ed's going biking round Africa. For charity."

"Wow," said Norm's mum. "That's **amazing!**"

"Yes, it is, isn't it?" gushed Auntie Jem.

"Isn't that **amazing**, love?" said Norm's mum.

"What?" said Norm. "I mean, pardon?"

"I said isn't that **amazing?** Your cousin, Ed. Biking round Africa for charity."

Norm pulled a face.
"What? **All** of it?"

Auntie Jem
laughed.
"No, not **all**
of it."

Norm was getting more fed up. And he'd been pretty fed up to begin with. How was **he** supposed to know that Auntie Jem hadn't actually meant that Ed was biking round **all** of Africa? What was he? Flipping psychic, or something? And anyway, it wasn't **such** a stupid question. Surely Africa wasn't **that** big, was it? Or maybe it was. Anyway, it didn't matter. What mattered was that Norm was getting increasingly cheesed off being treated like a complete and utter doughnut. Much more of **this** and he was going to blow a flipping fuse.

"Wait for me!" said a voice.

Norm turned round to see Becky running towards them. He hadn't even noticed that she'd stayed behind in the house, till now. No doubt she'd been busy brushing up on her rocket science, or maybe doing a spot of prize-winning hoovering.

"Hi," she panted, slowing down and walking alongside them once she'd caught up. Which was a pity, as far as Norm was concerned, because he'd been hoping she might just carry on running straight past.

"What have you been up to, Becky?" asked Auntie Jem. "Working on your novel?"

"Novel?" said Norm's mum, clearly impressed.

"Mum!" said Becky. "Do you *have* to tell everybody?

Yes, thought Norm. Auntie Jem *did* have to tell everybody. That was the whole flipping point of bragging!

"You're writing a *novel*, Becky?" said Norm's mum. "Wow!"

"Actually, she's already had interest from a literary agent," cooed Auntie Jem.

"Really?" said Norm's mum. "That's *wonderful*, Becky!"

"Yes, as a matter of fact, it *is* wonderful," said Auntie Jem. "Apparently she shows a lot of potential."

Yeah, thought Norm. Potential for making him want to throw up.

"What's it about?" said Norm's mum.

"It's about time we went home," muttered Norm under his breath.

"What was that, Norman?" said Auntie Jem.

"Nothing," said Norm.

"Go on, Becky," said Auntie Jem. "Say what it's about."

"I'd rather not say *too* much," said Becky.

Good, thought Norm. **He'd** rather Becky didn't say too much either. In fact, he'd rather Becky didn't say **anything** at all. But there wasn't much chance of **that**. Not with Auntie Jem around.

"Go on, Becky," said Auntie Jem. "Just a flavour."

A **flavour**? thought Norm. What was this? A novel, or a flipping cookery book?

"Well," said Becky. "It's about love. It's about life. It's about death."

Gordon flipping Bennet, thought Norm. A book about **death**? Why on earth would anyone in their right mind want to read **that**? He'd sooner read a mountain biking magazine any day! In fact, never mind a mountain biking magazine, he'd sooner read an instruction manual for a flipping washing machine any day. In **Norwegian**!

"I think it sounds great, Becky," said Norm's mum. "Don't you, love?"

"What?" said Norm. "I mean, pardon?"

"I think Becky's novel sounds great, don't you?"

"Erm..."

Becky smiled sweetly. "It's OK, Norman. You don't need to say if you don't want to. It's probably not your cup of tea."

Auntie Jem shot Norm a disapproving glance. But he'd just noticed something else instead. A dot in the distance that was gradually getting bigger and bigger. A dot that was rapidly heading their way. A dot that eventually turned out to be Mikey on his bike.

"Hi, Norm!" said Mikey skidding to a halt. "Fancy seeing you here!"

"Yeah, fancy," muttered Norm.

Mikey looked at Norm. "What's up?"

What was **up**? thought Norm. What was **up**? Did Mikey really need to ask? And what was he doing in this part of town, anyway? Trying to make him feel even **worse**? Not that Mikey had actually known Norm was going to be here, of course. But even so.

"Going for a bike ride, Mikey?" said Norm's mum.

"Yeah," said Mikey.

"Oh, of course," said Norm's mum, glancing in Norm's direction. "Sorry. I forgot."

Norm sighed. **He** flipping hadn't.

"You know Norman's Auntie Jem, don't you?" said Norm's mum, as if she was trying to change the subject. "And his cousin Becky?"

"Hi," said Mikey with a wave of a hand.

"Hello, Mikey," said Auntie Jem.

"Hi," said Becky.

"Becky's writing a novel, aren't you, Becky?" said Norm's mum.

Becky nodded.

"Cool," said Mikey. "What's it called?"

"**Knitting** Fog," said Becky.

Norm pulled a face. "So it's about knitting as well, then?"

"No," laughed Auntie Jem. "It's a metaphor."

Norm didn't care **what** it was for. He just needed to talk to Mikey. Alone.

"You coming, love?" said Norm's mum, setting off with Auntie Jem.

"In a minute, Mum," said Norm.

"OK," said Norm's mum. "Bye, Mikey."

"Bye," said Mikey.

"Bye, Mikey," said Becky following.

"Bye," said Mikey. "Good luck with the novel."

"Creep," said Norm watching them go.

Mikey pulled a face. "I was just being nice."

"You don't **honestly** think it's cool that she's writing a novel, do you?"

"Erm, yeah. I do actually," said Mikey.

"Knitting **frogs**?"

"Fog," said Mikey.

"Whatever," said Norm. "Still sounds rubbish."

"I think it sounds quite interesting, actually," said Mikey.

"Seriously?"

said Norm.

Mikey nodded.

"I bet it doesn't even have any pictures."

Mikey laughed.

"What?" said Norm.

"Not *all* books have *pictures*, Norm!"

"Mikey?"

"Yeah?"

"You're weird."

Mikey smiled.

"Sorry," said Norm.

Mikey shrugged. "It's OK. I've been called worse."

"What?" said Norm. "No, I'm not sorry about calling you weird. You *are* weird, Mikey. I'm sorry about not coming biking."

"Oh, right," said Mikey. "I tried to call you."

"Yeah, I know," said Norm. "I couldn't call back."

"It's fine, Norm. Honest."

"I really wanted to come," said Norm.

"I know you did," said Mikey.

They looked at each other for a moment.

"So," grinned Mikey. "You been having fun?"

"Have I been having **fun?**" said Norm.

Mikey nodded.

"Are you **serious?**"

But Mikey didn't reply. He was looking at something over Norm's shoulder.

"I'd have had more fun watching flipping paint dry."

"Er, Norm, there's..."

"In fact," said Norm, "I'd have had more fun watching someone **else** watching flipping paint dry."

"Norm," said Mikey, beginning to get quite agitated. "There's..."

"No, wait," said Norm cutting him off. "Trust me, Mikey. This is a good one. I'd have had more fun watching a documentary **about** someone watching someone else watching flipping paint dry! **That's** how much flipping fun **I've** been having!"

"Sorry to hear that?" said a voice.

Norm swivelled around to come face to face with his oldest cousin.

"Oh, hi, Ed. I wasn't talking about today. Er, obviously. Me and Mikey here were just talking about..."

"About what?" said Ed.

"An Xbox game," said Norm, blurting out the first thing that happened to pop into his head.

"Really?" said Ed.

"Weren't we, Mikey?" said Norm.

"Weren't we what?" said Mikey.

"Talking about an Xbox game and not anything else?"

"Er, yeah," said Mikey. "I mean, no. I mean..."

"Which game?"

"*Mortal Wombat*," said Norm.

"*Mortal **Wombat?**" said Ed.

Norm nodded.

"Hmm. Doesn't *sound* much fun."

"It's not!" said Norm emphatically.

"You should try the new *Call Of Mortal Combat*?" said Ed.

"I **know** I should," said Norm.

"It's, like, totally awesome?"

"I know it is," said Norm. "Well, actually I **don't** because I never actually got the chance to **play**, worse flipping luck."

Ed nodded. "I feel your pain?"

Yeah, right, thought Norm. What did Ed know about feeling flipping pain? **He** didn't have to live in a ridiculous little house and eat supermarket own-brand Coco Pops, did he? And did he **really** have to make every single thing he said sound like a flipping question?

"Cool bike by the way?" said Ed.

"What?" said Mikey. "Oh, right. Thanks."

"I suppose my mum's told you?" said Ed turning to Norm.

"About you biking round Africa?" said Norm. "Yeah, she's told me."

"Hmm," said Ed. "Thought she might have done?"

"Whoa!" said Mikey, clearly impressed. "You're biking round **Africa?**"

Ed nodded.

"What? **All** of it?"

"Don't be a doughnut, Mikey!" said Norm. "Of **course** he's not biking round **all** of it! It's **way** too big!"

"Yeah, s'pose so," said Mikey. "Hey, maybe you'd like to come biking with me and Norm some time?"

Norm shot Mikey a look. Was he **mad**?

"Cool," said Ed. "Where do you guys ride?"

Norm shrugged. "Just the woods behind the precinct and stuff."

"That sounds awesome?" said Ed.

"Well, I'd better leave you guys to it, then," said Mikey.

"Thanks **very** much, Mikey," said Norm, looking daggers at his best friend as he began to pedal off, leaving him alone with Ed

"See ya!" called Mikey. "Wouldn't want to be ya!"

Ed watched Mikey as he cycled off into the distance.

"He's funny."

"Yeah," said Norm. "He's, like, totally hilarious?"

CHAPTER 9

The good news, as far as Norm was concerned, was that they set off for home as soon as they got back from the walk. No cups of tea for the adults, no free-range organic cola, or prize-winning cake for the kids. Just straight in the car and off.

"Bye!" said Danny, waving them off from the bottom of the drive.

"Missing you already," muttered Norm under his breath.

The **bad** news, as far as Norm was concerned, was that if he thought the stink in the car was bad on the way to his perfect cousins', it was **nothing** compared to the stink on the return journey. Norm had smelled some horrific whiffs before, but never anything quite **this** horrific. In fact, in the unlikely event that a fairy godmother had magically appeared and granted him just **one** wish, it would have been that he never had to smell anything like it ever **again**. Not that a fairy godmother with any sense would have come anywhere near the car in the first place. Not without full breathing apparatus, anyway.

"Can you go any faster, Dad?" said Norm.

"Excuse me?" said Norm's dad. "**What** did you just say, Norman?"

Norm pulled a face. "I said can you go any faster?"

"That's what I **thought** you said," said Norm's dad.

So why flipping ask, then? thought Norm.

"I **can** go faster. But I'm not **going** to go faster."

"Uh?" said Norm.

"There **is** such a thing as a speed limit, you know?" said Norm's dad.

"Yeah, I know, but..."

"But, what, Norman?" said Norm's dad, the vein on the side of his head immediately beginning to throb. "I'm not going to break the speed limit and that's all there is to it!"

Norm sighed and wafted a hand in front of his face.

"What?" said Brian. "It's not **me!**"

"It's not **me**, either!" said Dave.

"Yeah, well it's not flipping **me**, either!" said Norm.

"Language," said Dave.

"Shut up, Dave!" hissed Norm.

"What's going on, back there?" said Norm's mum turning around.

"Norman thinks I've done a bottom burp," said Brian.

"No, I don't," said Norm. "I just think you **stink**, Brian."

"Charming," said Brian. "Anyway it's not me that stinks. It's John."

Woof! went John.

"Good **boy**, John!" cooed Brian.

"What's so good about **stinking?**" said Norm. "It's disgusting!"

"What?" said Brian. "No, I said 'good boy' because he recognised his **name!**"

"Big flipping deal," muttered Norm.

"It *is* a big deal, actually," said Brian. "He still can't speak English properly."

"No, Brian," said Norm. "He still can't **speak** full flipping stop! He's a dog, you doughnut!"

Dave giggled.

"You know what I mean," said Brian.

"No, I don't, actually," said Norm even though he knew perfectly **well** what Brian meant. He meant that John's **previous** owners were Polish and that therefore John only used to be able to understand **Polish** dog commands. And he didn't used to be called John either. But who **cared**? thought Norm. John stank in **any** flipping language. Which was quite appropriate, really, seeing as how he was actually a cock-a-poo and looked more like a toilet brush than a flipping dog.

Norm's mum sniffed a couple of times. "He **is** a **bit** stinky, isn't he?"

A **bit** stinky? thought Norm. John stank like nothing on **earth**. Or, at least, nothing on earth that hadn't already been dead for several weeks. Honestly, his mum must have something wrong with her sense of smell if she couldn't flipping smell what **he** was flipping smelling!

"He can't help it," said Brian. "He kept jumping in puddles!"

"Yeah, but puddles of **what?**" said Norm. "Wildebeest diarrhoea?"

"**Wildebeest** diarrhoea?" said Dave screwing his face up. "There aren't any wildebeest round here!"

"Stupid dog."

"John's not stupid," said Brian.

"Yeah, he is," said Norm. "Stupid **and** smelly."

"No, he's **not**."

"Yeah, he is," said Norm. "I'm going to put him in the washing machine when we get back."

Brian looked genuinely horrified. "What?"

"You heard," said Norm.

"You wouldn't dare."

"Wouldn't I?" said Norm. "Wanna bet?"

"MUUUUUUUUM?" yelled Brian. "NORMAN SAYS HE'S GOING TO PUT JOHN IN THE WASHING MACHINE WHEN WE GET BACK!"

"No, I **didn't**," said Norm indignantly.

"YEAH, YOU DID!" yelled Brian.

"Well, Norman?" said Norm's mum.

"Well, what?" said Norm.

"Don't answer your mother back!" said Norm's dad.

"But..."

"*Or* me!"

"But..."

"I said **don't** answer back!" snapped Norm's dad. "Did you, or did you not say you were going to put John in the washing machine when we got back?"

"I might have done," said Norm. "I can't remember."

"You can't **remember?**" said Norm's mum doubtfully.

"HE DID, MUM!" yelled Brian. "HONEST!"

"Shut up, Brian!" said Norm.

"WELL, YOU DID!"

"I was only joking."

"Ah, so you *did*, then?" said Norm's mum.

Norm sighed. "All right, all right. Yeah, I did."

"So why did you say you didn't, then?"

Norm shrugged. "Dunno, I just did."

"What have I told you about not answering your mother back?" said Norm's dad.

Gordon flipping Bennett,

thought Norm. What was he supposed to say *now*? Because if he said anything at all, wasn't he technically, answering back? It was so flipping confusing!

"Apologise," said Norm's dad.

"Who to?" said Norm.

"Your mother."

"Sorry, Mum," said Norm.

"What about **me**, Dad?"
said Brian. "He should
apologise to me as well!"

"What for?" said Norm.

"For **upsetting** me!"

"Well?" said Norm's dad.
"Go on, Norman."

Norm sighed. "Sorry, Brian."

"And John," said Brian.

"What do you mean **and** John?"

"I mean apologise to him," said Brian.

"You're joking, right, Brian?" said Norm. "You seriously expect me to apologise to a flipping **dog?**"

"Of course," said Brian.

"For threatening to put it in a washing machine?"

"**Him**," said Brian. "Not **it**."

WOOF! went John.

"Good **boy**, John!" said Brian.

Flipping typical, thought Norm. Anybody would think it was **him** who'd jumped in a puddle. Anybody would think it was **him** sitting there in the car, honking to high heaven. It wasn't even **his** flipping dog! Technically, John belonged to his **brothers**. But somehow it was still **him** who ended up having to say **sorry**! As flipping usual.

Well, as flipping usual ever since his stupid little brothers had been born, anyway. Everything had been fine up until then, thought Norm bitterly. He could literally do no wrong in his parents' eyes before Brian and Dave turned up to wreak havoc and wreck his life forever. He could have accidentally blown the flipping house up and his mum and dad would have just laughed it off as some kind of childish prank gone wrong. But not any more. Oh no. Now **every** little thing was somehow **his** fault. No matter **how** small. No matter how ridiculous. No matter whether Norm was even flipping **there** or not. He **always** seemed to get the flipping blame! And it just wasn't flipping fair. It just wasn't flipping fair at all!

Norm stared out the window. The houses were gradually getting smaller and smaller again. It wouldn't be long before they were home now.

But that was OK. In fact, in a weird kind of way Norm was actually quite looking forward to getting back home. He might not have *Call Of Mortal Combat*. He might not have a den and a screen the flipping size of **Denmark**. But at least he wouldn't be made to feel inferior because he had a rubbish phone. At least he wouldn't be looked down on because he wasn't writing some stupid book about flipping fog or something. And at least he'd get some decent grub inside him, that didn't look like it had been discovered in a flipping skip!

"Well, Norman?" said Norm's dad. "We're all waiting."

"What for?" said Norm.

"For you to say sorry to John."

Norm sighed. "Sorry, John."

John immediately jumped up and started licking Norm full in the face.

"AAAAAAAAAARGH!" yelled Norm. "GET HIM OFF ME!"

"Here we are, boys!" said Norm's mum as they turned into their street. "Home sweet home!"

Not a moment too flipping soon either, thought Norm. Much more of this and he was going to barf.

CHAPTER 10

Norm was straight out on his bike just as soon as he'd washed his face and sprayed himself from head to foot with Stynx. Not that **that** did much good. He could **still** smell John and was pretty sure he'd be able to for the rest of his life.

As usual, within seconds, Chelsea had popped up on the other side of the fence. How did she flipping **do** that? wondered Norm. More importantly, perhaps, **why** did she flipping do that? To deliberately wind him up and annoy him? Because if so, it worked every flipping time! Not that Norm was **ever** going to tell her that, of course. She'd be even **more** unbearable than usual. And **that** was flipping saying something.

"Hello, **Norman?**"

Norm decided not to reply. If he didn't say anything then maybe she'd get bored and go away.

"HELLO, NORMAN!" said Chelsea a bit louder.

Norm sighed. So much for **that** flipping theory, then.

"All right?"

"**I'm** all right," said Chelsea. "The question is, are you all right?"

"Not really, no."

"Oh, that is a shame. Would you like to talk about it?"

"Not really, no."

"Did you have a nice walk with your cousins?"

"Not really, no," said Norm.

"Oh dear," said Chelsea. "This conversation's going *nowhere*, **Norman**."

Good, thought Norm. Because **nowhere** was precisely where he was **hoping** the conversation was going. Now if she'd just leave him in peace for five minutes and let him...

"Why the long face?"

"What?" said Norm.

"You look fed up."

"Oh, right," said Norm. "Yeah, well, I suppose I am, really."

"Why?" said Chelsea.

Gordon flipping Bennet, thought Norm. If he **told** her would she shut up **then**? Probably not. It was worth a try, though.

"My cousins."

"You're fed up because of your cousins?" said Chelsea.

"Basically," said Norm.

"What's so bad about them?"

"What **isn't?**" said Norm.

"Hmm," said Chelsea. "**That** bad, eh?"

Norm nodded and started practising bunny hops.

Chelsea looked puzzled. "What are you doing?"

"Practising bunny hops."

"**Bunny** hops?" laughed Chelsea. It looks like

you're just jumping up and down on your bike to me."

Norm sighed. "I **am**. It's called bunny hopping."

"Oh, I see," said Chelsea. "What's the point of **that?**"

Gordon flipping Bennet, thought Norm. What was the point of bunny hopping? What was the point of **Chelsea**? Apart from to ask stupid flipping questions? Because as far as Norm could see, there wasn't one.

"It's just something you need to be able to do."

Chelsea grinned. "Speak for yourself, **Norman!**"

Norm wobbled and nearly fell off his bike. What was **supposed** to have been a nice relaxing time on the drive, honing his biking skills and generally chilling out was rapidly turning into the complete **opposite** of all that. And it was all flipping **Chelsea's** fault. Why couldn't she just leave him alone?

"So?"

"So, what?" said Norm.

"Are you going to tell me what's so bad about your cousins, or am I going to have to guess?"

Norm looked at Chelsea for a moment. She really **wasn't** going to let this go, was she?

"You really want to know?"

Chelsea nodded. "I really want to know."

"They've got this Xbox game."

"Yeah?"

"Yeah," said Norm.

"And?" said Chelsea.

"I really want it, too."

"I see," said Chelsea. "Which one is it?"

"Uh?"

"Which game, **Norman?**"

What was the point? thought Norm. Chelsea would never even have **heard** of it. She was bound to be far more interested in stupid games about keeping pets and designing your own house and **interacting** with people and all that other girly kind of stuff. Not games about giant robot squid taking over the earth.

BEEP WHIRR

"Well?" said Chelsea.

Norm shrugged. "You wouldn't know it."

"Try me," said Chelsea.

"*Call Of Mortal Combat*."

"*Call Of Mortal Combat?*"

"Yeah," said Norm.

"The brand new one?"

"What?" said Norm.

"The one that only came out at midnight last night?"

Norm pulled a face. "Er, yeah."

Chelsea grinned. "Got it."

Norm stared at Chelsea for a moment. Had he momentarily switched off and not heard properly? Had someone crept up and poured custard in his ears without him noticing? **Chelsea** had got the brand new *Call Of Mortal Combat?*

Chelsea? The most annoying part-time next door neighbour a guy could ever wish for? Or rather, the most annoying part-time next door neighbour a guy could **never** wish for? It just wasn't possible. She **had** to be joking. She just **had** to be flipping **joking**. Because if she wasn't, thought Norm, he was going to seriously have to think about moving house again. With **or** without the rest of his family.

"Erm, did you say you've...?"

"Got the brand new *Call Of Mortal Combat* on Xbox?" said Chelsea. "Yep. I believe I did."

This, thought Norm, wasn't just unbelievable. This was **unbe-flipping-lievable**. As well as staggeringly unfair, obviously. But that almost went without saying, as **most** things in Norm's life were staggeringly unfair, as far as **he** was concerned. This was merely the latest in a long **list** of staggeringly unfair things that would stretch from earth to the flipping **moon** and back, if he could actually find a piece of paper long enough.

Staggeringly Unfair Things

"You look surprised," said Chelsea.

"Do I?" said Norm as nonchalantly as possible. Which wasn't very easy considering he was feeling anything **but** flipping nonchalant. He was actually feeling completely **un**chalant. Or whatever the opposite of nonchalant was.

"Don't you want to know how come I've got it?"

"Not really," lied Norm.

"My dad queued up for it," said Chelsea, telling him anyway.

"Right," said Norm.

Chelsea looked at Norm as if she was expecting him to say something else. Or as if she was **hoping** he'd say something else, anyway.

"Have you played it yet?"

"Are you serious?" asked Chelsea. "Have I **played** it?"

Norm nodded.

"Of **course** I've played it, Norman! I've been playing it all day! What do you take me for?"

Norm thought for a moment. What did he take Chelsea for? The jammiest flipping doughnut in the entire history of jammy flipping doughnuts! **That** was what he flipping took her for!

"It's **awesome!**" said Chelsea.

"Is it?" said Norm still desperately trying to give the impression that he couldn't care less.

Chelsea looked puzzled. "You mean you didn't actually **play** it?"

Norm sighed. "I **wish**."

"Why not?"

"Because we had to go on a stupid flipping **walk**, didn't we?" said Norm.

"Ah," said Chelsea. "Bad luck."

Bad luck? thought Norm. It was more than bad luck. It was...it was...it was...

"You can borrow it if you want?"

"What?" said Norm.

"You can borrow it," said Chelsea.

If Norm had been amazed to discover that Chelsea **owned** a copy of *Call Of Mortal Combat*, he was completely and utterly gobsmacked to find out that she was actually prepared to **lend** him it.

"Only if you want to, though," said Chelsea. "You don't **have** to."

This, thought Norm, was what was commonly known as a dilemma. Because, on the one hand, of **course** he wanted to borrow it. He was abso-flipping-lutely **desperate** to get his hands on a copy of the brand spanking new *Call Of Mortal Combat*! Who in their right mind **wouldn't** be? It was a complete no-brainer. On the **other** hand, the **last** thing he wanted to do was to borrow it from **Chelsea**. Because if he did **that**, he was going to have to be **grateful** to her. And **that** was a prospect too awful to even think about. But then, even as Norm **wasn't** thinking about it, he suddenly thought of something else. **Why** was Chelsea offering? What was in it for **her**? Because there **had** to be something. There certainly would be if it was the other way round and Norm was offering to lend **Chelsea** the most sought after computer game on the planet! Yeah, thought Norm. Like **that** was ever likely to happen!

"What are you thinking?" said Chelsea.

"Nothing," said Norm. "Just..."

"What, **Norman?**"

"Why?" said Norm.

"Why am I offering to lend it to you?"

Norm nodded.

"My mum wouldn't let me play it at hers," said Chelsea. "So I'm just going to leave it here at my dad's and play at weekends."

"Right," said Norm.

"And tomorrow's Monday. So **you** might as well borrow it, **Norman**."

Norm looked at Chelsea.

"What?" said Chelsea. "You think I have some kind of ulterior motive?"

"Some kind of **what?**" said Norm.

"You think I've got some other **reason** for lending it and that it's all part of some cunning plan?"

"Erm, well…"

"Well, I haven't," said Chelsea. "And actually that's quite hurtful. I just thought you might like to borrow it, that's all. But if you don't want to, that's…"

"No, no, I'll have it!" said Norm quickly. "I mean, I'll borrow it!"

Chelsea eyed Norm for a couple of seconds.

"What do you say?"

"Please?" said Norm, gritting his teeth so hard that they practically hurt.

Chelsea eyed Norm for a couple *more* seconds.

"I'll *think* about it."

"What?" said Norm.

Chelsea laughed. "It's OK, **Norman**. You can have it! Wait there a minute."

Norm watched as Chelsea trotted off into her

dad's house.

"Has she left you?" said a voice.

Norm turned around to see Grandpa walking up the drive.

"Oh hi, Grandpa," said Norm. "Has **who** left me?"

"Your girlfriend," said Grandpa with a nod of his head towards Chelsea's house. Or rather, Chelsea's **dad's** house.

"Chelsea's **not** my girlfriend, Grandpa!" said Norm. "I don't know **how** many times I've told you!"

"Who is, then?"

"What?" said Norm.

"Who **is** your girlfriend?"

Norm sighed with exasperation. "I don't **have** a

girlfriend, Grandpa! All that stuff's totally gross and disgusting!"

"You won't be saying that in a couple of years," said Grandpa.

"I flipping **will**," muttered Norm.

"I heard that," said Grandpa. "And by the way, you flipping **won't**."

Norm and Grandpa looked at each other. Grandpa's eyes crinkled ever so slightly in the corners. It was the closest he ever came to smiling.

"Here you are, **Norman!**" said Chelsea reappearing at the fence, holding a plastic box. "Did you miss me?"

"Hello, young lady," said Grandpa.

"Oh, hi!" said Chelsea sweetly. "Didn't see you there!"

"Ah, that's because I move in mysterious ways."

Uh? thought Norm. What was Grandpa on about? Moving in mysterious ways? What was he? A flipping **crab** or something?

"Didn't know you were coming, Grandpa," said Norm.

"Neither did I," said Grandpa.

"What?" said Norm.

"I was just passing. Thought I'd pop in and say hello to my favourite grandson."

"Ah, that's nice," said Chelsea.

"Where *is* Brian, by the way?" said Grandpa.

"Yeah, yeah, very funny, Grandpa," said Norm.

"He knows I'm only joking," said Grandpa turning to Chelsea. "And anyway, Dave's my favourite."

Chelsea burst out laughing. But Norm had heard it all before.

"What's that you've got there, by the way?" said Grandpa.

"Oh, you mean this?" said Chelsea. "It's an Xbox game."

"An Xbox game, eh?" said Grandpa. "What's it called?"

"*Call Of Mortal Combat.*"

"*Call Of Mortal Combat*, eh?" said Grandpa.

Gordon flipping Bennet, thought Norm. Grandpa had better not say that **he'd** queued up all night to flipping get it, as well! Because if he did, Norm was going to go abso-flipping-lutely **mad**!

"Have you heard of it, Grandpa?" said Norm.

"Can't say I have, no," said Grandpa.

Thank goodness for that, thought Norm.

"I've heard of Xbox, though."

"You should let your grandpa have a go, **Norman**," grinned Chelsea.

"Oh, I don't know about **that**," said Grandpa.

"Trust me. It's **awesome!**" said Chelsea.

"Awesome, eh?" said Grandpa.

"Totally," said Chelsea. "You could play each **other!**"

"Hmm," said Grandpa stroking his chin thoughtfully. "What do you think, Norman?"

It was a good question actually, thought Norm. What *did* he think? It was more fun playing *with* someone than by yourself, that was for sure. And it wasn't as if he was going to be able to play with one of his little brothers, was it? Or his parents! Because *they* weren't to even know Norm had *borrowed* Call Of Mortal Combat which was going to be tricky for a start, what with the TV and the Xbox being in the front room.

"Well?" said Grandpa.

Norm shrugged. "Why not?"

"Excellent," said Grandpa. "In that case, let *Call Of Mortal Combat* commence!"

"What? Right now, Grandpa?" said Norm.

"Well, once I've had a cup of tea, anyway," said Grandpa.

"Here you go, **_Norman_**," said Chelsea handing the game over the fence.

"Thanks," said Norm.

"Don't mention it!" said Chelsea. "Enjoy!"

Norm smiled. Oh he was going to enjoy it all right. There was no doubt about that. No doubt whatso-flipping-ever.

CHAPTER 11

As it turned out, it wasn't in the least bit tricky for Norm to play *Call Of Mortal Combat* without his mum and dad knowing, because pretty much as soon as he went back into the house, his mum and dad went to the supermarket to do the big weekly shop. That meant Norm had a good hour or so to do whatever he wanted. The only downside was that because Grandpa had suddenly turned up out of the blue, Brian and Dave could be left at home. Even so, Norm could hardly believe his luck. And it wasn't very often ***that*** happened!

And as it turned out, Chelsea was right. *Call Of Mortal Combat* really **was** pretty flipping awesome. Not that that came as a major surprise to **Norm**, of course. Frankly just about **anything** was going to seem pretty flipping awesome compared to the kind of games he was usually allowed to play, which in Norm's opinion were more suitable for someone nearly thirteen **months** old and not someone nearly thirteen **years** old, like he was.

"Gotcha!" said Grandpa as he blew Norm's last remaining intergalactic supply ship to pieces.

"Aw, Grandpa!" said Norm. "What did you have to go and do **that** for?"

"It's a dog eat dog world out there, Norman," said Grandpa. "Deal with it."

Norm looked at Grandpa for a moment. Dog eat dog world? What on earth did **that** mean? And how come Grandpa was so flipping good at *Call Of Mortal Combat*, anyway? Old people weren't **supposed** to be good at Xbox games! But then, thought Norm, Grandpa wasn't **like** most old people. Or, at least, not like most old people **he'd** met, anyway, who generally just moaned and sucked mints all day and went on about stuff that happened about three thousand years ago.

"Are you sure you've not played this before, Grandpa?"

"Hmm, let me see now," said Grandpa. "No, I don't think so."

"You don't **think** so?" said Norm, wondering how exactly you could play a game about earth being invaded by giant robot squid and then forget all about it. "What Xbox games **have** you played, then?"

"I haven't played **any**," said Grandpa. "This is my first time."

Norm couldn't help laughing.

"What's so funny?"

"**You** are, Grandpa," said Norm.

"Cheeky monkey," said Grandpa, the corners of his eyes crinkling ever so slightly.

Norm laughed again. It really was great spending time with Grandpa, **especially** after the kind of rubbish day **he'd** had. And **especially** when it involved staring at a screen with an Xbox controller in his hand! Usually when he saw Grandpa it was at the allotments. And let's face it, thought Norm, there was only so much fun you could have with a watering can and a wheelbarrow.

"What did you *use* to play, Grandpa?"

"What's that?" said Grandpa, narrowly avoiding being shot by one of Norm's zombifying laser rays.

"What did you use to play?" said Norm. "When you were my age?"

"Oh, we used to make our own entertainment back then."

"Really?" said Norm, wondering how it was possible to actually *make* an Xbox, let alone any games to play on it.

"Of course," said Grandpa.

"But..."

"What?"

"Nothing," said Norm, deciding it best not to say anything that was likely to upset or offend Grandpa. Not if he wanted Grandpa to keep playing, anyway.

"I know what you're thinking, Norman."

"Do you, Grandpa?"

"I'm not *that* old, you know. We had electricity when *I* was a boy as well."

Norm looked genuinely surprised. "Really?"

"Yes, *really!*" said Grandpa.

Norm thought for a moment. "What about television?"

"What about it?"

"Had it been *invented* when you were a boy?"

"Had it been *invented?*" said Grandpa raising his cloud-like eyebrows. "Of *course* it had been invented!"

"Right," said Norm.

"Mind you, there *were* only two channels to watch in those days."

Norm pulled a face. Had Grandpa just said what he *thought* he'd just said?

"Only *two* channels?"

"I know," said Grandpa. "Hard to believe, isn't it?"

Hard to believe? thought Norm. It was almost *impossible* to believe! Nowadays there were literally *hundreds* of channels to choose from. OK, so *most* of them were completely unwatchable, like The Ironing Channel and The Extreme Cake channel, or whatever. But even so, if *Norm*

only had two flipping channels to choose from he'd be straight on the phone to Childline.

"You just killed me, by the way," said Grandpa.

"What?" said Norm distractedly.

"You just killed me."

"Oh, yeah," said Norm. "Sorry, Grandpa."

"No need to apologise, Norman. All's fair in love and war."

Uh? thought Norm. What was Grandpa on about **now**? Where did he **get** these expressions from?

"You just killed Grandpa?" said a voice.

Norm spun round to see Brian standing in the doorway, looking horrified.

"What?"

"You just **killed** Grandpa?"

"Uh?" said Norm. "Not **really**, Brian, you idiot. He's right here!"

"Oh yeah," said Brian. "Hi, Grandpa."

"Greetings, earthling," said Grandpa in a funny voice.

"What's that you're playing?"

"*Call Of Mortal Combat*," said Norm.

"But..." began Brian.

"What?" said Norm.

"Do Mum and Dad know?"

"Erm..."

"I'm telling," said Brian.

"Brian?" said Norm.

"Yeah?"

"Don't even *think* about it."

"But..."

"I said, don't even think about it," said Norm menacingly.

"But..."

"Brian?"

"Yeah?" said Brian.

"If you tell, I really *will* put your stupid smelly dog in the washing machine."

Brian looked at Norm for a moment, his bottom lip instantly beginning to quiver.

"I don't believe you."

"I couldn't care less if you believe me, or not."

No one said anything for a few seconds. The only sound that could be heard was the sound coming out of the TV – a mixture of whooshing lasers, pounding heavy metal music and exploding robot squid.

"Have you two finished?" said Grandpa eventually.

"Finished what?" said Norm.

"Bellyaching like a couple of constipated cows."

Brian pulled a face. "Cows are *girls*, Grandpa!"

"Shut up, Brian, you little freak!" hissed Norm.

"I'm telling," said Brian.

"Telling what?" said Norm.

"That you called me a 'little freak'," said Brian.

"Oh, right," said Norm. "I don't mind you telling about *that*. And anyway, you *are* a little freak."

"That's your opinion," said Brian.

"No," said Norm. "It's a fact."

Brian stood and watched as Norm and Grandpa continued to play.

"Don't let me keep you, Brian," said Norm.

"What?" said Brian.

"Clear off."

"Charming," said Brian indignantly. "I know when I'm not wanted."

Norm snorted. "No, you flipping **_don't!_**"

"What do you mean?" said Brian.

"If you knew when you weren't **_wanted_** you wouldn't have come in here in the first flipping place!"

"OK, OK, I'm going," said Brian, turning round and leaving.

"Do you not think that was a bit harsh?" said Grandpa, once Brian had disappeared again.

Norm shrugged. "Not really, no."

"By the way, you didn't tell me you weren't **_supposed_** to be playing this."

Norm shrugged again. "You didn't ask."

"Why not?" said Grandpa.

Norm pulled a face. "I've no idea why you didn't ask, Grandpa."

"No, I meant why aren't you supposed to be playing this?"

"Oh, right, I see," said Norm. "Because my mum and dad don't approve of me playing games about killing things."

Grandpa frowned until his eyebrows very nearly met in the middle. "Not even giant robot squid?"

"Not even giant robot squid."

"Seems a bit unreasonable," said Grandpa.

Norm sighed. "Welcome to my world."

They carried on playing for a while before Norm had a thought.

"You won't say anything, will you, Grandpa?"

"What do you mean, I won't say anything?"

"To my mum and dad?"

"About what?"

"Playing *Call Of Mortal Combat*?"

"Why would I tell your mum and dad that I've been playing *Call Of Mortal Combat*?" said Grandpa. "It's none of their business. I can do what I want."

Gordon flipping Bennet, thought Norm. It was like they were talking different languages.

"No, Grandpa. I meant you won't say anything about **me** playing *Call Of Mortal Combat*! Not **you**!"

"Oh, I seeeee," said Grandpa. "Hmmm..."

And what was *that* supposed to mean? wondered Norm.

"What's it worth?"

"What?" said Norm.

"What's it worth?" said Grandpa. "To keep schtum?"

Schtum? thought Norm. Now they really *were* talking entirely different languages!

"To keep quiet," said Grandpa as if he could read Norm's mind.

Norm couldn't quite believe what he was hearing. Was he being *blackmailed*? By his *own* grandpa? Because if he was, that was bang out of order, thought Norm, conveniently forgetting that he himself wasn't averse to using blackmail in the right circumstances – or even in the *wrong* circumstances.

"Are you **serious**, Grandpa?"

"Of course I'm not serious, you big daft numpty," said Grandpa, his eyes crinkling in the corners.

Norm exhaled slowly and noisily. He had to hand it to Grandpa. He'd really had him going for a minute there. Well, maybe not a minute. But a couple of seconds, anyway.

"Sorry, Norman. Couldn't resist it."

"It's OK," said Norm. Even though it wasn't. "What do you think, by the way?"

"What do I think about what?"

"*Call Of Mortal Combat*," said Norm.

"Oh, right, I see," said Grandpa. "It's most agreeable."

172

"Uh?" said Norm.

"It's, like, totally **awesome**, dude!" said Grandpa.

Norm laughed. **Now** they were talking the same language!

Grandpa suddenly sniffed a couple of times like he'd only just noticed a really bad smell.

"Phwoar."

"What?" said Norm.

"I don't know what it is, but **something** stinks like the inside of a sumo wrestler's jockstrap."

Norm sniffed a couple of times. The Stynx obviously wasn't **quite** as long-lasting as it said on the can. There was no alternative. This called for drastic action. It was time for a bath.

CHAPTER 12

It wasn't **every** day Norm had a bath without being told to. Then again, it wasn't **every** day Norm discovered that he stank like the inside of a sumo wrestler's jockstrap. Not that Norm had the faintest idea what the inside of a sumo wrestler's jockstrap actually smelled like. Which begged the question, how come **Grandpa** knew what the inside of a sumo wrestler's jockstrap **smelled like**? Had he ever got close enough to one to find out? And if so, **why** had he? Was Grandpa in fact a secret sumo wrestler in his spare time? When he wasn't working on his allotment, obviously. But that wasn't the point, thought Norm, stripping off his clothes

and wrapping a towel around his middle. The point was that, despite almost using an entire can of Stynx, he still stank like a rhino's rear end. And he needed to do something about it. And quickly. Which was precisely why he'd run himself an extra deep, extra **bubbly** bath.

As Norm padded along the landing towards the bathroom he could hear Grandpa talking to his mum and dad, who by now were back from their trip to the supermarket. Norm couldn't quite make out what they were actually talking **about** down there, but whatever it was, he knew that he could rely on Grandpa not to spill the beans about playing *Call Of Mortal Combat* He and Grandpa had a special kind of bond. They'd shared secrets before. They'd **confided** in each other before. Told each other stuff that they probably wouldn't have told anybody else before. Heck, Norm had **even** talked about his **feelings** to Grandpa before. And Norm **hated** talking about his flipping **feelings** more than just about anything! So as far as **Norm** was concerned, Grandpa's lips would be well and truly sealed.

Closing the door behind him, Norm hung his towel up and looked at the bath for a moment. It really was **very** bubbly indeed. But that was a good thing. It meant he could just lie there and get nice and clean simply by soaking, instead of going to all the trouble of actually **washing** himself. Brilliant, thought Norm, climbing in and gently lowering himself into the water.

Lying in the bath, all his cares quickly began to dissolve and evaporate. Well, not **all** his cares. Norm would have had to spend the next **week** in the bath for **all** his cares to dissolve and evaporate. But before long, **several** of his cares had begun to dissolve and evaporate. It was a start, though.

Norm studied the bubbles, imagining that they were a range of snow-capped mountains. A range of snow-capped mountains just begging to be biked down. Biked down at great speed. Quickest one wins. And the winner gets crowned World Mountain Biking Champion! One of these days, thought Norm wistfully. One of these flipping days.

Norm was so busy daydreaming that at first he didn't notice one of the 'mountains' beginning to move. And when he eventually **did** notice, he didn't think too much of it and just imagined that one of the 'mountains' was actually a volcano about to erupt. Little did Norm know that it was actually **him** who was about to erupt.

"AAAAAAAAAAAAAAAAAAAGH!" screamed Norm, as John poked his head up out of the bubbles, like the sun rising majestically above the horizon. Except that the sun didn't have a stupid grin all over its stupid face, or its tongue lolling about like a wet sock on a washing line.

"GET OUT!" yelled Norm dementedly.

Not only did John **not** get out of the bath, he continued to stare at Norm as if he thought that if anything, it was **Norm** who should be getting out the bath – and not the other way round.

"RIGHT! THAT'S IT!" said Norm, suddenly lunging forward and grabbing John before dropping him, dripping wet over the side and onto the bathroom floor.

WOOF! went John, making a beeline for the toilet brush.

"Uh? What? NOOOOO! STOP!" yelled Norm when he realised what was happening.

But it was too late. John was already trotting happily back towards the bath with the toilet brush clenched firmly between his teeth as if it was a stick.

Norm watched in ever increasing horror as John leapt and landed back in the bath with a huge, bubbly splash.

"AAAAAAAAAAAAAAAAAGHH! THAT'S DIS-FLIPPING-GUSTING!" shrieked Norm. "GIVE IT HERE!"

John did no such thing. Furthermore he looked like he had no intention whatsoever of doing any such thing, prompting Norm to lunge forward again and grab the brush.

"I SAID, GIVE IT HERE, YOU FURRY FLIPPING FREAK!" said Norm, shaking the brush – and John – vigorously from side to side, causing more and more water to spill out of the bath and onto the bathroom floor.

Eventually, though – and after much shaking – John let go of the toilet brush. Unfortunately, so did Norm, sending the brush arcing through the air, before landing, with a horrible inevitability, straight in the toilet.

"Don't even think
about it," said Norm.

But again it was too late. John was out the bath
like a shot.

"PLEASE, NOOOOOOOO!" yelled Norm as the
soggy cock-a-poo retrieved the toilet brush from
the toilet and headed back towards the bath like
this was the greatest game ever.

Gordon flipping Bennet! thought Norm as John
landed back in the bath with **another** huge,
bubbly splash. How much more gross could things
actually **get**? The answer, it turned out, was **much**
more gross.

"AAAAAAAAAAAAAAAAAGH!" screamed Norm,
as John jumped up and started pawing him on his

chest. Which was bad enough at the best of times, but what with also having a stinky toilet brush being waved about, mere millimetres from his nose, it was more than Norm could bear, and he jumped out the bath like a shot.

"WHAT'S GOING ON IN THERE?" shouted Norm's dad from outside the bathroom door, as Norm stood in an ever expanding puddle of water on the bathroom floor.

"Er, nothing, Dad," said Norm, looking around at the mess.

"LET ME IN!"

"What?" said Norm, desperately stalling for time.

"YOU HEARD!" yelled Norm's dad. "LET ME IN!!!"

Norm sighed. He knew that he was going to have to let his dad in **sooner** or later. And he knew that whenever he did, **he** was going to get the blame. Just like he always flipping **did.**

WOOF! went John.

Norm turned around and noticed that John was still staring at him.

"What are **you** flipping looking at?"

WOOF! went John again.

Norm glanced in the mirror and immediately realised **exactly** what John was looking at. He was completely naked.

"HURRY UP, NORMAN!" yelled Norm's dad.

"Coming, Dad!" said Norm grabbing his towel and wrapping it around his middle. He hated to admit it, but at that precise moment, Norm was actually just a teensy bit grateful to John. Without him, things could have been even worse than they were already. And **much** more embarrassing!

Norm opened the bathroom door.

"Yes, Dad?" said Norm innocently.

Norm's dad stood in the doorway and gawped, his jaw almost hitting the ground as he surveyed the scene inside.

"Is there a problem?" said Norm.

"Is there a **problem?**" said Norm's dad, the vein on the side of his head immediately beginning to throb. "Look at the **state** of this place, Norman! It's...it's... it's..."

"Good **boy**, John!" cooed Brian, appearing in the doorway.

WOOF! went John from the bath, looking just about as pleased with himself as it was possible for a dog to look.

Uh? thought Norm. Had the whole flipping world gone mad and no one had bothered to tell him?

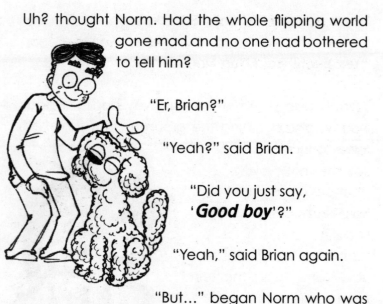

"Er, Brian?"

"Yeah?" said Brian.

"Did you just say, '*Good boy*'?"

"Yeah," said Brian again.

"But..." began Norm who was genuinely struggling to find the right words. Or **any** words, for that matter.

"What?" said Brian. "He **is** a good boy. Aren't you, John?"

WOOF! went John again, jumping out of the bath, before shaking himself dry and showering Norm in the process.

"OI!" yelled Norm. "STUPID FLIPPING DOG!"

"He's **not** stupid!" said Brian crossly. "He's very clever. And you're lovely and clean now too, aren't you, boy? Yes, you are!"

Norm pulled a face. "What? You mean..."

"Well, he's had his bath now, hasn't he?"

Norm looked at his middle brother in astonishment, making a mental note to google whether the world had indeed gone mad. It was the only possible explanation.

"Erm, did you say...**his** bath?"

"Uh-huh," said Brian nodding.

"**John's** bath?"

"Yeah, why?"

"But..."

"What?" said Brian.

"That was **my** bath," said
Norm.

Brian looked surprised.
"Oh. Was it?"

"Gordon flipping Bennet," said
Norm. "Yes, it **was** actually."

"I thought someone had run it for John, Dad!
Honest!"

"Don't worry about it, Brian," said Norm's dad.

"What?" said Norm incredulously. "Are you serious,
Dad?"

"Of course I'm serious, Norman. It's not **Brian's**
fault, is it?"

Flipping typical, thought Norm. Being blamed for something he hadn't actually done! The only surprise was that this could **still** come as a surprise! It happened so often you'd think he'd be used to it by now. "Please tell me you're joking, Brian? You honestly thought the bath was for **John?**"

Brian shrugged. "Well, he was really stinky! Yes you were, weren't you, John?"

WOOF! went John.

"But you're not any more, are you?" said Brian in a funny baby voice. "No, you're not because you've had a lovely bubbly barfy-warfy, haven't you? Yes, you have!"

"Yeah, he flipping hassy-wassy," said Norm. "**My** flipping barfy-warfy!"

"Aw, don't listen to him, John. He's just being silly-willy!"

Unbelievable, thought Norm. Just unbe-flipping-lievable.

"Oops, sorry, Dad," said Brian. "Didn't mean to say that."

"Say what?" said Norm's dad.

"Silly-willy," said Brian. "Anyway, Norman, I think you'll find it's Mum and Dad's bath."

"What are you on about, Brian?" said Norm. "Mum and Dad aren't going to have a bath together! At least I flipping **hope** not!"

"What was that, Norman?"

"Er, nothing, Dad."

"What I **meant**," said Brian, "was that technically speaking, the bath **belongs** to Mum and Dad. Just like everything else in the house."

"Shut up, Brian, you little freak!" said Norm, still desperately trying to erase any last, lingering thoughts of his mum and dad in the bath at the same time.

"Don't speak to your brother like that, Norman," said Norm's dad.

Norm pulled a face. "Like **what?**"

"Like **that!**" said Norm's dad, the vein on the side of his head beginning to throb more and more strongly.

"Yeah, Norman," said Brian.

Norm glared at Brian. Brian stuck his tongue out at Norm.

"And by the way, you're banned from the Xbox."

"What?" said Norm. "Who is?

"You are."

"WHAT?" said Norm.

"You heard," said Norm's dad.

Norm's dad was right. Norm **had** heard. He just couldn't quite **believe** what he'd heard, that was all. Banned from the Xbox? What for?

"For making all this mess," said Norm's dad, saving Norm the bother of having to ask.

"But..."

"No buts, Norman. You're banned from the Xbox and that's all there is to it."

Norm sighed with resignation. But he knew there was no point arguing. He could see that his dad had made his mind up. Nothing that Norm said now was going to change it. **Everything** was **his** flipping fault, same as flipping **always**.

"Well, I'd better be off then, I suppose," said Brian.

Yes, thought Norm. You'd flipping **better**.

"Come on, boy!" said Brian heading towards the stairs.

WOOF! went John scampering out the door.

"How long, Dad?"

"How long what?" said Norm's dad.

"Am I banned from the Xbox for?"

"Oh, till next weekend."

"Next **weekend?**" shrieked Norm. "That's…"

"What?" said Norm's dad.

Norm had stopped himself in the nick of time. He knew full well that if he said what he **really** wanted to say, he'd get banned for even longer.

"Quite reasonable under the circumstances."

"Good," said Norm's dad. "That's settled then."

Hmm, thought Norm. **That** might be settled. But there was something **else** that would have to be settled now. A score. With Brian. Because if Brian honestly thought he was going to get away with this then he had another flipping think coming.

"Better get this sorted, hadn't you?"

Norm looked at his dad for a moment. "Get **what** sorted?"

"The **mess**, Norman. What do you **think** I mean?"

"But..."

"I said no buts, didn't I?"

"Yeah, but..." began Norm. "I mean, yeah."

"Well, then," said Norm's dad turning to leave. "What are you waiting for?"

Norm took a deep breath and let it out again slowly and noisily. What was he *waiting* for? He was waiting for the flipping world to become a fairer flipping place to live in. Or at least for *his* world to become a fairer flipping place to live in.

Yeah, thought Norm. Like *that* was ever going to happen.

CHAPTER 13

The rest of the day – what was left of it – had passed Norm by in a bit of a blur. A blur of doom and gloom and general despondency, with a side order of deep-fried bitterness and simmering resentment thrown in for good measure. Banned from the Xbox? For something that wasn't actually *his* fault? Flipping typical!

If Norm was hoping that the *next* day was going to be any *better*, his hopes were quickly dashed.

"Time to get up, love!" said Norm's mum, knocking on Norm's bedroom door before opening it.

"Uh? What?" yawned Norm, scarcely having the energy to raise *one* eyelid let alone two.

"Time to get up."

"Why?"

"Because you have to get ready for **school**, that's why!" said Norm's mum.

"Uh?" said Norm.

"It's **Monday**, love!"

"What?" muttered Norm. "Gordon flipping Bennet."

"Don't tell me you'd **forgotten?**" laughed Norm's mum.

All right, then, I won't, thought Norm rolling over and snuggling back into his duvet. And what difference would it make, anyway, if he **had** forgotten? None whatso-flipping-ever. He was going to have to go to school whether he liked it or not. And just for the record, thought Norm, he flipping well **didn't** like it.

"Bring your laundry down with you, please," said Norm's mum, turning to leave.

"What?" said Norm.

"Your dirty clothes?" said Norm's mum. "Bring them downstairs and put them in the basket!"

"'Kay, Mum."

"**Before** you have your breakfast!"

"**'Kay**, Mum."

"Don't forget!" yelled Norm's mum, heading down the stairs.

Gordon flipping Bennet, thought Norm. Do this, do that. It was like being a flipping **servant** in one of those really boring programmes his parents liked to watch on TV. The ones about posh people living in whacking great houses, talking all funny and wearing dead weird clothes. Except, of course, that they didn't actually **have** washing machines back then. Then again, thought Norm, they actually had hardly **anything** back then. No mobile phones, no iPads. And **definitely** no Xboxes! Imagine **that**. No wonder people in paintings from the olden days always looked so flipping miserable.

Norm sighed. He'd just reminded himself. People in the olden days weren't the **only** ones without Xboxes. **He** didn't have an Xbox either. Well, he **did**. But he wasn't allowed to flipping play on it. Not till the next weekend he wasn't, anyway. Just when he'd got hold of a copy of *Call Of Mortal Combat* too. And he was going to have to give it back to flipping Chelsea next weekend. If he wanted to play it after **that** he was actually going to have to **suggest** going to see his perfect flipping cousins! And frankly, thought Norm, there was more chance of him selling his **bike** than there was of him actually **suggesting** going to see his perfect flipping cousins. And there was more chance of him giving **birth** than there was of him ever selling his bike.

Norm winced. What on earth was he doing, thinking about giving birth? Which reminded him – he really needed to go to the toilet.

"Morning, Norman," grinned Dave, appearing in the doorway with an armful of clothes.

"What's so funny?" grumbled Norm.

"Enjoy your bath last night, did you?"

"Oh, I see," said Norm. "So you heard about that, did you?"

"You'll laugh about it **one** day," said Dave.

"Huh," snorted Norm derisively. "You reckon?"

"Well, that's what Grandpa always says."

Norm thought for a moment. Dave was right. Grandpa **did** always say that. It was just hard to imagine a time when Norm would ever look back on accidentally sharing a bath with a stinky dog and having a flipping bogbrush waved under his nose and find it even **remotely** amusing. He knew one thing, though. It wouldn't be happening any time soon.

"Where is he, anyway?" said Norm.

"Who?" said Dave. "Grandpa?"

"No, you doughnut," said Norm. "Brian!"

"Who wants to know?" said Brian, appearing next to Dave and also bearing an armful of clothes.

Norm pulled a face. "What do you **mean** who wants to know? *I* want to know, you little **_freak!_** What do you think this is, Brian? Some kind of flipping movie?"

"No," said Brian.

"Well, shut up, then," said Norm.

"Charming," said Brian.

"Freak," said Norm.

"I'm fine thanks, by the way."

"I didn't ask," said Norm.

"I know you didn't," said Brian.

Norm groaned. He really couldn't be bothered with all this. Not at this time of the morning, he couldn't. Or **any** time of the morning, for that matter. He just wanted to be allowed to wake up in his own sweet time. Preferably **without** a flipping audience! And how come Brian was so cocky and full of himself, anyway? If anything, he was being even **more** annoying than usual! And **that** took some flipping doing. Surely he knew that it was only a matter of time before he paid the price for yesterday? He didn't honestly think Norm was simply going to **forget** all about it? Or did he?

"HURRY UP, BOYS!" yelled Norm's dad from the bottom of the stairs.

"Coming, Dad!" shouted Dave.

"AND DON'T FORGET YOUR WASHING!"

"Got it, Dad!" shouted Dave.

"What?" said Brian to Norm.

"What do you mean *what?*" said Norm.

"You're looking at me all funny."

"Am I, Brian?" said Norm. "I hadn't noticed."

"Well, you wouldn't, would you?" said Dave.

"Wouldn't what?" said Norm.

"Notice if you were looking at someone all funny. *They'd* notice. But *you* wouldn't."

"Uh? What?" said Norm.

"Oh, I get it!" said Brian. "This is about the Xbox, isn't it?"

"Might be," said Norm, doing his best to sound mysterious and slightly sinister at the same time.

"I bet you think it's **my** fault, don't you?"

Norm looked at Brian in utter disbelief.

"What do you mean, you bet I **think** it's your fault? It **is** your flipping fault, Brian!"

Brian shrugged. "So what are you going to do about it?"

"Erm..."

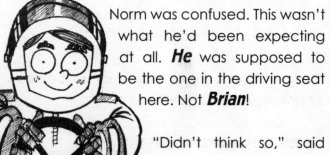

Norm was confused. This wasn't what he'd been expecting at all. **He** was supposed to be the one in the driving seat here. Not **Brian**!

"Didn't think so," said Brian.

"What do you mean?" said Norm.

Brian smiled. "Aren't you forgetting something, Norman?"

Norm thought for a moment. He couldn't remember if he was forgetting something or not.

"Our...little secret?" said Brian.

Gordon flipping Bennet, thought Norm, as the penny finally dropped and he suddenly remembered what he'd forgotten. Brian had walked in on him and Grandpa playing *Call Of Mortal Combat* the day before and now...

"What little secret?" piped up Dave, derailing Norm's train of thought.

"Shut up, Dave," said Brian.

"Yeah, shut up, Dave," said Norm. "So what are you saying here, Brian?"

"Yeah, what **are** you saying here, Brian?" said Dave.

"SHUT UP, DAVE!" said Norm and Brian together.

"Right, I'm telling," said Dave, heading for the stairs.

Norm and Brian looked at each other for a few seconds.

"Well?" said Norm expectantly.

"It's very simple," said Brian. "You do **anything** to me and I tell Mum and Dad."

"NORMAN? BRIAN? GET DOWN HERE, NOW!" yelled Norm's dad from the hall. "AND BRING YOUR DIRTY WASHING WITH YOU!"

"Coming, Dad!" said Brian heading for the stairs.

Norm sighed. Credit where credit was flipping due. Brian had clearly thought this through. Which was more than **he'd** done. And now it looked like he was going to have to go back to the drawing board. Wreaking some kind of horrible revenge on Brian himself was out of the question now. He was obviously going to have to be a little bit more subtle. It was **SO** flipping annoying.

CHAPTER 14

Still no more than half awake, Norm slouched into the utility room carrying his washing, tripped up on something and landed in a heap on the floor. The **good** news, as far as Norm was concerned was that it was a heap of other peoples' washing. So at least it was a nice soft landing and he didn't hurt himself. The **bad** news, as far as Norm was concerned, was that it was Brian and Dave's washing and therefore extremely smelly.

"Phwoar," said Norm, extracting himself from a particularly pongy pair of pants and picking himself up off the floor.

WOOF! went John from his basket.

Norm turned around and sighed. So **that's** what he'd tripped up on. No flipping wonder! There wasn't enough room to swing a flipping **cat** in this place, let alone a flipping **dog**! Of course this would **never** have happened in their **old** house. Not that they'd actually **had** a flipping dog in their old house. But that wasn't the point. The point was they'd had a proper, decent-sized utility room in their old house. Not like now. But then **everything** was tinier now. Like they lived in a flipping **doll's** house or something. And a really **small** doll's house at that!

"Everything all right in there, love?" shouted Norm's mum from the kitchen.

"No, it flipping **isn't!**" mumbled Norm.

"What was that?"

Norm sighed. "Nothing, Mum. Everything's fine!"

"Good," said Norm's mum appearing in the doorway. "In that case, put the washing on for me, would you, please?"

"What?" said Norm, like he'd just been asked to teach a llama how to belly dance.

"Put the washing on please. I'm busy."

Norm pulled a face. His **mum**? Busy? All she did was sit around all day ordering useless stuff from shopping channels. Or, at least, she **did** before his dad got sacked and they were skint all the flipping time. Now she mostly just **looked** at shopping channels, dreaming about all the useless stuff she could order if they weren't so flipping skint!

"Doing what?"

Norm's mum looked at Norm.

"Are you serious?"

Norm shrugged. "Yeah."

"Making your breakfast."

Norm thought for a moment. "You mean getting cereal out the cupboard?"

"**And** I'm trying to get your brothers ready for school. And I'm trying to get ready myself!"

"What for?"

"What *for?*" said Norm's mum. "What do you mean, what for?"

"Why have **you** got to get ready as well?"

"For work," said Norm's mum.

"What? Oh, yeah," said Norm, who'd forgotten his mum had a part-time job in a cake shop.

"**Someone** in this family's got to."

"Yeah," said Norm.

"So if you **could** put the washing on..."

"But..."

"What?" said Norm's mum.

"I don't know **how**, Mum! I've never actually done it before."

"You've never put the washing on before?" said Norm's mum. "How old are you, Norman?"

Norm looked at his mum. Well, if **she** didn't know how old he was...

"It's very simple, love. All you need to do is load it into the machine, close the door, put some powder in the little drawer, turn the dial on the left to 3, the dial on the right to 40 and press 'start'."

"What?" said Norm, as if his mum had suddenly started speaking Mandarin.

"Oh and make sure you don't accidentally put any woollens in because you'll ruin them."

"Uh?" said Norm.

"You need to wash woollens separately, love, otherwise they'll shrink."

Norm pulled a face. "But..."

"Just do your best. Any problems, get Brian to help you. Gotta go!"

"Really?" said Norm in disbelief. "*Brian?*"

"Or Dave," said Norm's mum, heading off. "And hurry up or *you'll* be late too!"

Norm sighed. He didn't have the faintest idea what his mum had been on about. Not only that, but he still had no idea *why* he should have to do it, anyway! What *was* this? The flipping army, or something? And why couldn't his stupid little brothers do it if they were so flipping clever? And how come *they* knew how to work the washing machine and *he* didn't? thought Norm. If it wasn't so flipping annoying he might actually be quite insulted!

Norm began to sense that he was being watched.

"What are **you** looking at?" he said glaring at John.

WOOF! went John.

"Stupid flipping dog," muttered Norm turning his attention to the pile of washing on the floor.

What was that his mum had said? You needed to wash woollens **separately** or else they'd **shrink**?

The idea hit Norm without warning. Not exactly like a bolt from the blue. More like a gentle kick up the backside. Suddenly Norm knew **_exactly_** how he could get his own back on Brian for getting him banned from the Xbox. **_Without_** being too obvious. **_Without_** it looking like a deliberate act of cold blooded revenge. And crucially, **_without_** Norm immediately being labelled as prime flipping suspect!

First of all, though, there was something he needed to do. And quickly.

"Whoa! Where do you think **_you're_** going?" said Norm's dad as Norm zoomed through the kitchen, almost knocking him off his feet.

"TOILET!" yelled Norm. "CAN'T STOP!"

"You're not going to play on the **_Xbox_**, are you, Norman?" grinned Brian from the kitchen table. "Oh no, of course. I've just remembered. You're **_banned_** from the Xbox, aren't you?"

Norm couldn't help smiling to himself as he bounded up the stairs two at a time. Because if everything went to plan, it would be **_him_** having the last laugh, not Brian.

CHAPTER 15

Rather than heading for the bathroom, Norm headed straight for Brian and Dave's room instead and quickly closed the door behind him. He knew he had to move fast if he didn't want to get caught. And Norm really ***didn't*** want to get caught. Not if everything was to go smoothly he didn't, anyway. But where to begin? thought Norm, looking around. The chest of drawers seemed like as good a place as any.

It proved to be an inspired choice. Norm found precisely what he'd been looking for before he could say Gordon flipping Bennet. Not that he actually ***did*** say Gordon flipping Bennet because he didn't want anyone to

know he was in there. But if he **had** tried to say Gordon flipping Bennet there wouldn't have been time. Amidst all the Spiderman pyjamas, the dinosaur socks and the X-Men pants, there it was. Brian's **favourite** jumper. His so-called **precious** jumper. The one with the slimy little *Nerd of the Rings* guy on the front, that his perfect cousin, Becky had knitted from free-range, underprivileged sheep, or whatever. Well, it wasn't **Brian's** precious any more. It was **Norm's**.

Stuffing the jumper beneath his own, Norm closed the drawer, opened the door and emerged onto the landing just as Dave was coming up the stairs.

"What have you been **doing**, Norman?"

"Going to the toilet."

"In my room?" said Dave suspiciously.

214

"Er, yeah," said Norm. "Got lost, didn't I?"

Dave looked at Norm doubtfully. "**Lost?**"

Norm nodded.

"How can you get *lost* in your own house?"

Norm shrugged. It wasn't **all** that long since he'd done precisely that and got lost in his own house and ended up almost peeing in his dad's wardrobe.

"Dunno, just did."

"No, really," said Dave. "What **have** you been *doing*?"

"Really?"

"Really," said Dave.

Norm sighed. Dave was nothing if not persistent. He clearly wasn't going to let this go until he got an answer that he was truly satisfied with.

"I, er…was looking for something."

"I see," said Dave. "And did you…**_find_** that something?"

"Er, yeah, I did," said Norm.

"And is that it, there?"

"Where?" said Norm.

"There," said Dave with a tilt of his head. "Underneath your jumper."

Norm pulled a face. "Didn't think it was that obvious."

Dave grinned. "It is if you're **_my_** height."

"It's not yours, Dave."

"What isn't?"

Norm hesitated. "Whatever it is that's under my jumper."

"I see," said Dave. "So it's **Brian's**, then, is it?"

Norm shrugged. "Might be."

"What are you going to do with it?"

"Can't say," said Norm.

"**Can't** say, or **won't** say?" said Dave.

Gordon flipping Bennet, thought
Norm. It was like being cross-
examined in court. Not that he'd
ever **been** cross-examined in
court. But honestly. Perhaps it
would be better to just **tell**
Dave what he was up to
and get it flipping over with.

"Well?" said Dave.

"Long story," said Norm.

"Fair enough," said Dave.

"What?"

"Well, if you don't want to tell me, I can't very well **make** you, can I?"

"So..."

"I don't want to know," said Dave heading for the bathroom.

Blimey, thought Norm. This wasn't what he'd been expecting at all. He was **assuming** Dave was going to attempt to blackmail him in some way. Or at the very least threaten to tell his mum and dad. Not that he was complaining, of course. Far from it. But it just went to show. His brothers weren't incredibly annoying **all** the time. Well, **one** of them wasn't, anyway.

"Dave?" said Norm.

"Yeah?" said Dave without turning round.

"Can I go in there before you?"

"In your dreams," said Dave closing the bathroom door behind him.

CHAPTER 16

"You did **what?**" said Mikey in disbelief, as he and Norm walked round the school playing field that lunchtime.

"You heard," said Norm.

"You **deliberately** put Brian's favourite jumper in the washing machine so that it would shrink?"

"Correct," said Norm.

"Because it's his fault you're banned from the Xbox?"

"Abso-flipping-lutely!" said Norm. "See? Told you you'd heard, Mikey."

"But..." began Mikey.

"What?" said Norm.

"That's..."

"What?" said Norm again.

Mikey hesitated, as if he wasn't quite sure whether to say what was on his mind or not.

"Well, it's a bit..."

"A bit **what**, Mikey?" said Norm beginning to get irritated.

"A bit harsh."

Norm stopped. Mikey followed suit. They both looked at each other for a moment.

"Harsh?" said Norm.

Mikey nodded.

"**Harsh?**" said Norm again, as if he hadn't seen Mikey nod and he was just making sure.

Mikey nodded again.

"I'll tell you what's flipping **harsh**, Mikey," said Norm. "Getting punished for something that's not your flipping **fault! That's** harsh!"

"Hmm," said Mikey. "I guess so."

Yeah, thought Norm. And that was **all** Mikey would **ever** have to flipping do. **Guess** so. Because Mikey was something that Norm could now only ever **dream** of being. An **only** child. Mikey would never actually **know** what it was like to have incredibly annoying little brothers or sisters, bugging the heck out of him and threatening to tell his mum and dad if he so much as farted.

MUM?

"But still…"

Norm pulled a face. "What do you **mean**, but still, Mikey? There **is** no flipping but still! Honestly, you have no flipping idea what it's like! He's had it coming for a long time."

"**How** long?" said Mikey.

Norm thought for a second. How old was Brian? "Ten years."

"But..."

"What?"

"That's as long as Brian's been alive!"

"Yeah, exactly," said Norm. "What's your point?"

Mikey laughed.

"It's not funny, Mikey!"

"Sorry, Norm."

They resumed walking round the playing field, an awkward silence hovering over them like a bad smell.

Sllence

"Talking about the Xbox..." began Mikey.

"Must we?" said Norm.

"Sorry, Norm."

"Go on," said Norm. "You've started now."

"I was just going to say..."

"What, Mikey?"

"Ed's right."

"What do you mean?" said Norm.

"Your cousin?" said Mikey.

"I **know** who Ed is, Mikey! What do you mean he's right? Right about **what?**"

"*Call Of Mortal Combat*," said Mikey. "It really **is** awesome."

Norm stopped again and turned slowly to Mikey. "What did you just say?"

"Erm, I said it's... it's...it's..."

"Mikey?"

"Yeah?"

"Have you **got** *Call Of Mortal Combat*?"

"Erm, well..."

Norm hardly dared ask. But he knew he had to. "The new one?"

"Erm, well..."

Norm sighed. "Unbe-flipping-lievable."

"Sorry, Norm," said Mikey sheepishly. "I wasn't…"

"What?" said Norm.

"Thinking," said Mikey.

Mikey was right, thought Norm. He **wasn't** flipping thinking. He'd obviously just been trying to make conversation. He'd just blurted it out and hadn't really thought things through. If he had he would never have said it in the first place. Because if there was one thing that Mikey wasn't, that one thing was boastful. And nasty. And unkind. OK, thought Norm, so that was three things. But Mikey wasn't any of them.

"The thing is…" began Mikey.

"The thing is," Norm interjected, "is that it's fine, Mikey."

Mikey looked surprised. "What?"

"Well, I mean it's not **your** fault, is it?"

"What's not?" said Mikey.

Norm shrugged. "That my life's completely unfair?"

"Erm, well…"

"Well, I mean it's not, is it?" said Norm. "Any more than it's **my** fault that you're a complete and utter jammy doughnut!"

Mikey looked sheepish.

"S'pose so."

"It's just the way it goes, Mikey."

"Yeah, I know, Norm, but even so…"

"What?"

Mikey sighed. "I shouldn't have said."

"What?" said Norm. "That you've got the brand new *Call Of Mortal Combat*?"

Mikey looked at the ground and nodded.

"It's OK. I was bound to find out sooner or later," said Norm.

"Yeah, s'pose."

"Just wish it had been later."

"Fancy playing on it sometime, Norm?" said Mikey as the bell rang, signalling the end of lunch and the beginning of afternoon lessons.

"Mikey?" said Norm.

"Yeah?"

"Do bears fart in the forest?"

"What?" said Mikey.

"Of **course** I fancy playing sometime, you flipping doughnut! What kind of stupid question's **that?**"

They looked at each other. Norm grinned. Mikey grinned back. They both knew it would take more than this to destroy their friendship. It was a blip, that was all. An annoying flipping blip, as far as **Norm** was concerned. But a blip nevertheless.

"I'd love to see his face when he finds out."

Norm was confused. "Uh? What? Who's face?"

"Brian's!" said Mikey. "When he sees his jumper!"

"Oh, right!" said Norm as the penny dropped. **He** was looking forward to that, too. **Really** looking forward to it.

"See you, then, Norm," said Mikey heading off in one direction.

"Yeah, see you, Mikey," said Norm heading off in another.

CHAPTER 17

"Is that you, love?" called Norm's mum as Norm closed the front door behind him.

"No," said Norm, chucking his school bag on the floor.

"Don't answer back!" called Norm's dad. "And pick that **up!**"

Gordon flipping Bennet, thought Norm, doing as he was told and hanging his bag on a hook. How did his dad **know**? Was he watching him on CCTV or something? Did he have an app on his phone? Did his dad even **have** a flipping phone?

"We're in here, love!"

"Where?" said Norm.

"Here," called Norm's dad.

Well that's cleared **that** up, thought Norm. Not that you needed to be a great detective to work out where someone was in this stupid little house. Or even need to be a **rubbish** detective.

"Hi," said Norm's mum as Norm slouched into the front room.

"Hi," said Norm.

"Good day?"

Norm shrugged. "Not particularly."

"That's a shame. Want to talk about it?"

Norm shrugged again. "Not particularly."

"Well, **we** had a very nice day, thanks for asking," said Norm's dad.

Norm sighed. So it was going to be like **that**, was it? In which case, the sooner his mum and dad said what they'd got to say, the sooner he could disappear up to his room and check out the latest biking videos on his iPad.

"Your father and I have been talking," said Norm's mum.

Alarm bells immediately began ringing in Norm's head. Firstly, his mum hardly **ever** referred to his dad as 'your **father**' – and when she did it was usually followed by bad news of one kind or another. Secondly – talking about **what**, exactly? Presumably not the weather or the price of flipping fish or something else incredibly boring. Because if they **had** been, why on **earth** would they then want to tell **him** all about it? No, thought Norm. One way or another this didn't look good at all. The

TV wasn't even on. And the TV was nearly **always** on. Especially when his mum was anywhere near it, with a credit card in her hand.

"So?" said Norm's mum when it was clear that Norm wasn't going to say anything himself.

Norm pulled a face. "What?"

"What do you mean **what?**" said Norm's dad.

"What?" said Norm.

Norm's mum looked at Norm for a moment. "Tell us about *Call Of Mortal Combat*."

Gordon flipping Bennet, thought Norm. Never mind **alarm** bells ringing in his head. Klaxons, sirens and flipping **foghorns** were going off so loud he could hardly hear himself think! The little so and so had flipping well grassed him up after all!

"What's he said?"

"What's **who** said, love?"

"Brian," said Norm.

Norm's mum looked puzzled. "Brian?"

Oops, thought Norm. Perhaps he'd been a bit too hasty jumping to conclusions. Maybe Brian **hadn't** snitched on him after all.

"Have you got something to say, Norman?" said Norm's dad.

"Er, no, Dad," said Norm a bit too quickly.

Norm's dad eyed Norm suspiciously. "Are you sure?"

Norm nodded. "Sure I'm sure, Dad. I was thinking of something else."

"Hmmm," said Norm's dad, clearly not convinced.

"So?" said Norm's mum.

"What?" said Norm. "I mean pardon? I mean, yeah, Mum?"

"Tell us about *Call Of Mortal Combat*."

"Oh, right," said Norm. "Erm well, it's a game."

"Yes, I know *that*," said Norm's mum. "But what *kind* of game?"

"Computer game," said Norm. "You know? Playstation? Xbox? Whatever?"

Norm's mum sighed. "Yes, I know *that* as well, love. But what's it *about?*"

"It's about forty quid," muttered Norm under his breath.

"What was that, Norman?" said Norm's dad, the vein on the side of his head beginning to throb ever so slightly.

"Er, I said it's about robot squid, Dad."

"Robot squid?" said Norm's mum.

Norm nodded. "That invade the earth. And you have to try and destroy them with lasers and stuff."

"Lasers?" said Norm's mum.

"Er, I think so," said Norm.

"You *think* so?" said Norm's dad. "You don't *know?*"

"How *should* I, Dad?" said Norm nervously. "I've not played it. Honest."

"I should hope not, either, love!" said Norm's mum. "You're too young!"

"Yeah, but..."

"No buts, Norman," said Norm's dad. "You're too young. End of. And anyway, what do you mean, you've not played it, *honest?* I didn't say you *had* played it, did I?"

"Yeah. I mean no. I mean..."

Norm was getting confused. **Had** Brian told on him or not? **Did** his mum and dad actually know about Chelsea lending him hers? Or had Grandpa accidentally let the cat out the bag and said something? If not, what was all this leading up to? Because one thing was certain. It was definitely leading up to **something**. And frankly, thought Norm, the sooner he found out what it was leading up to, the flipping better. Because this was beginning to do his head in.

"Did you know your **cousin's** got *Call Of Thingy*?" said Norm's mum.

"*Mortal Combat*?" said Norm.

Norm's mum nodded. "Yes, that."

"Which cousin, Mum?" said Norm, knowing full well who his mum meant.

"Danny."

"Really?" said Norm.

Norm's mum smiled. "You look surprised."

Norm was secretly quite chuffed. Because surprised was **precisely** what he'd been **trying** to look. He was obviously a better actor than he'd thought. But how come his **mum** actually knew that?

"I was chatting to your Uncle Steve today," said Norm's mum, as if she'd been reading Norm's mind. "He called into the shop."

"What shop?" said Norm.

"The one where I **work?**"

"Uh?" said Norm.

"The cake shop?" said Norm's mum. "Strictly Come Munching?"

"Oh, right!" said Norm finally twigging. "Why?"

"Why?"

"Yeah," said Norm. "Why would Uncle Steve call into a **cake** shop? I thought Becky would be like, World Baking Champion, or something."

Norm's dad had to stifle a laugh.

"What's so funny?" said Norm's mum.

"Nothing," said Norm's dad briefly making eye contact with Norm. "Just thought of something, that's all."

Norm's mum thought for a moment. "What was I saying?"

"About Uncle Steve calling into the shop?" said Norm.

"Oh yes," said Norm's mum. "Do you know he actually queued up for it? At **midnight?**"

"Yeah, I know," said Norm.

Norm's mum looked at Norm. "Pardon?"

"I mean, no, I didn't know, Mum," said Norm. "Why **would** I know that if I didn't know Danny had got it in the first place?"

Norm's mum nodded. "Fair enough."

Gordon flipping Bennet, thought Norm, getting increasingly confused. **Was** this leading up to something or not? Because he was beginning to flipping wonder. And it looked like he wasn't the only one either.

"Mind if I...?" said Norm's dad.

"Be my guest," said Norm's mum with a wave of her hand.

"Your mum and I were thinking of buying it for you."

Norm looked at his dad for a moment.

"What?"

"We were thinking of buying you *Call Of Mortal Combat*," said Norm's dad.

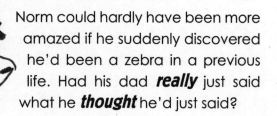

Norm could hardly have been more amazed if he suddenly discovered he'd been a zebra in a previous life. Had his dad *really* just said what he *thought* he'd just said?

"Sorry, Dad. Did you just say you were thinking of **buying** me *Call Of Mortal Combat*?"

"Only if you'd like us to?" said Norm's dad.

Only if he'd **like them to**? thought Norm. There

was abso-flipping-lutely **nothing** he wanted **more**, apart from being an only child again. But short of selling his brothers on eBay, there wasn't much chance of **that** happening in the near future.

"Well, love?" said Norm's mum.

"But..."

"What?" said Norm's dad.

"Why?" said Norm.

"Why?" said Norm's dad.

Norm nodded.

"Because..."

Because **what**? thought Norm. Because the planets were in alignment? Because there was an 'r' in the month? Because pigs had **finally** learned how to fly?

Norm's dad smiled. "We just thought it would make you happy, that's all."

Whoa, thought Norm. His parents were actually trying to make him **happy**? Perhaps pigs really **had** learned to fly after all!

"There **is** a catch," said Norm's mum.

Norm sighed. Of **course** there was a catch. There always flipping **was** a catch. He didn't honestly think his parents would just **buy** him *Call Of Mortal Combat* for the sheer **heck** of it, did he?

"What, Mum?"

"We can't afford to give you money for a brand **new** one."

"What?" said Norm. "But..."

"But what, love?"

"It's only just come out!"

"So?"

Gordon flipping Bennet! thought Norm. Wasn't it screamingly obvious?

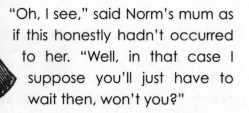

"There won't be any second hand copies yet!"

"Oh, I see," said Norm's mum as if this honestly hadn't occurred to her. "Well, in that case I suppose you'll just have to wait then, won't you?"

"Yeah, right," muttered Norm.

"What was that, Norman?" said Norm's dad.

"Er, I said yeah, I might, Dad."

"Oh and another thing," said Norm's mum. "When I say **give** you the money, what I actually mean is **lend** you the money."

"Uh?" said Norm. "You mean…"

"I mean it's just a loan, love. Exactly. But at least you're **getting** one!"

Yeah, thought Norm. **Eventually**. About a year from now or something. Just in time for the flipping **next** *Call Of Mortal Combat* to come out. It was almost as bad as not getting one in the first flipping place. But not quite.

"Remember I only work part-time," said Norm's mum. "It would be different if your dad had a job."

Norm sighed. His mum was right. It **would** be different if his dad had a job. But then a **lot** of things would be different if his dad had a job. They could afford to buy proper Coco Pops, for a start. **And** a proper flipping house!

"Is there a problem?" said Norm's dad.

Was there a **problem**? thought Norm. Flipping right there was a problem! Not only was there a **catch** as usual – there were actually **two** flipping catches! Getting a second hand copy of *Call Of Mortal Combat* and having to pay back the money afterwards? It wasn't just unfair – it was **doubly** flipping unfair! And, besides, thought Norm, where was **he** supposed to get the money to pay his mum and dad back? Because as his dad never **ever** tired of saying, money didn't grow on flipping trees.

UNFAIR + UNFAIR = DOUBLY Flipping UNFAIR!

"Oh, you're still banned, by the way," said Norm's dad.

"What?" said Norm.

"You're still banned from the Xbox."

Norm couldn't believe it. So now he wouldn't even be able to **play** it? Never mind **two** flipping catches – there were **three**! But before he could say anything else, there was a sudden, bloodcurdling scream from the direction of the kitchen.

"Brian?" said Norm's mum leaping off the sofa and rushing towards the door. "Oh my goodness, what's happened?"

Norm allowed himself a slight smile. He had a pretty good idea he knew what had happened. At least it wasn't **all** bad news.

CHAPTER 18

As Norm suspected, it turned out that the bloodcurdling scream didn't actually come from the kitchen itself, but from the so-called 'utility' room just **off** the kitchen.

"MY PRECIOOOOOOOOOOOOOOOOOOUS!" wailed Brian, clutching his beloved *Lord of the Rings* jumper to his chest as first Norm's mum, then Norm's dad and then finally Norm himself appeared in the doorway.

Norm's dad pulled a face. "Is it me, or has that shrunk a bit?"

"A BIT?" wailed Brian.
"LOOK AT IIIIIIIIIIIIIIIIIIIIT!"

Norm looked as Brian held the jumper up for everyone to see. It was fair to say that his cunning plan had worked. In fact, it was fair to say that his cunning plan had worked far better than he could ever **possibly** have imagined. The jumper had indeed shrunk. And not just a **bit**. It was about half the size it used to be. Either that, thought Norm, or Brian had suddenly got **much** bigger.

Norm's mum turned to Norm and sighed. "What have you **done**, love?"

Norm shrugged what he **hoped** would be interpreted as a perfectly innocent shrug.

"'Snot **my** fault."

Brian looked, open-mouthed at Norm for a moment, before turning to his mum.

"What do you **mean**, what's

248

he done, Mum?"

"Erm, well, the thing is..." began Norm's mum.

"The thing is, I haven't done **anything**, Brian," said Norm immediately on the defensive.

"But..."

"I asked him to put the washing on, because I was too busy," said Norm's mum.

"Yeah and that's what I did," said Norm.

"But I said not to put any **woollens** in, because they'd be ruined!"

Norm shrugged again. "I **didn't**."

"Well, **someone** did," said Norm's mum.

"Well, it wasn't me," said Norm.

"Well, it wasn't **me**, either!" said Brian.

"How do you know it wasn't?" said Norm.

"How do I know it wasn't **me** who ruined my own **favourite** ever jumper?"

Norm nodded again.

"I just know!" shrieked Brian.

"You might've done," said Norm.

"What?"

"You might've put your jumper in the pile by accident."

"Why would I do **that?**" said Brian getting more and more hysterical.

"Because you got it dirty yesterday," said Norm.

"Even if he **did** accidentally put it in the pile..." began Norm's mum.

"Which I **didn't!**" wailed Brian.

"But even if you **did**, Brian, **you** should have spotted it, love," said Norm's mum to Norm.

"Perhaps **you** should've done the washing yourself?" said Norm's dad.

"Excuse me?" said Norm's mum turning round and looking daggers at his dad.

"I just..."

"I was getting ready to go to **work!**" said Norm's mum angrily.

"Well, anyway, there's no point arguing about it now," said Norm's dad. "What's done is done."

Brian looked horrified. "What?"

"Dad's right," said Norm's mum gently.

"You mean..."

Norm's mum nodded. "It's ruined."

Everything went very quiet for a few seconds. The calm before the storm. Until eventually the storm broke.

"AAAAAAAAAAAAAAAAARGH!" wailed Brian, hugging his tiny shrunken jumper close to his chest. "MY PRECIOOOOOOOOOUS!"

By now, Norm was finding it extremely difficult not to break out into the biggest, cheesiest grin in the entire history of big, cheesy grins. The sight of Brian in bits was *almost* worth being banned from the Xbox in the first place.

"What's happened?" said Dave appearing in the doorway.

"There's been a little...accident," said Norm's mum.

"Accident?" said Dave. "I wondered what the smell was."

"That's the dog," said Norm.

WOOF! went John right on cue.

Dave pulled a face.

"Is it me, or has that shrunk a bit?"

"what? The dog?" said Norm.

"No," said Dave. "Brian's jumper."

"***That's*** the accident," said Norm's mum.

"Oh, I seeee," said Dave. "How did ***that*** happen?"

"That's what I want to know!" said Brian, glaring at Norm.

"What?" said Norm. "I told you, Brian. It's not **my** fault!"

WOOF! went John again.

"I think he's trying to say something," said Brian. "What was that, John?"

WOOF! went John looking directly at Norm. WOOF, WOOF, WOOF!

"Shut up, you furry flipping freak," hissed Norm.

Dave grinned at Norm.

"What?" said Norm.

"Nothing." Dave shrugged.

Norm had to admit it. For a seven year old, Dave was incredibly shrewd. He knew **exactly** how Brian's jumper had ended up shrinking in the wash. He knew **exactly** what had been under **Norm's** jumper that morning when they'd bumped into each other on the landing. He knew exactly what Norm had been up to. Not only **that**, thought Norm, but Dave **knew** that Norm knew he knew what he'd been up to. It was so flipping annoying. But then, as long as Dave didn't actually **say** anything to anybody, did it really **matter** if he knew that Norm knew that he knew what he'd been up to?

"Hey, I've got an idea," said Norm's mum. "The jumper's the right size for **you** now, Dave! **You** could have it!"

"What? And look like a complete **nerd?**" said Dave. "No offence, Brian."

"None taken," sobbed Brian.

"Don't suppose now would be a good time to mention that loan, would it?" said Norm, keen to change the subject before any more incriminating questions were asked. Never mind the fact that there wouldn't actually be any second hand copies of *Call Of Mortal Combat* yet. He needed to get out.

"Here, love," said Norm's mum, fishing a crisp twenty pound note out of her purse and handing it to Norm.

"Thanks, Mum," said Norm slipping the money into his back pocket and heading for the front door.

"Where are you going?" said Norm's dad.

"Games-R-Us," said Norm.

"Don't forget!" called Norm's mum as the front door slammed shut. "It's just a loan!"

But Norm didn't even **hear** his mum, let alone **reply**. He was already half way down the drive on his bike.

CHAPTER 19

As Norm pedalled furiously towards the precinct, he still couldn't quite believe he'd got away with it. But he obviously **had**. Otherwise why would his mum have given him the money?

The one **possible** fly in the ointment, thought Norm, whizzing past the supermarket, jumping the steps and skidding to a halt in front of Games-R-Us, was that **Dave** knew it hadn't been an accident. Dave knew perfectly well that Norm had **deliberately** put Brian's jumper in the washing machine so that it would shrink. But that might not **necessarily** be a problem. Not everyone automatically blabbed like a baby, did they? Come to think of it, thought

Norm, **Brian** hadn't actually blabbed to his mum and dad the night before when he'd discovered him and Grandpa playing *Call Of Mortal Combat*. Not that that had stopped Norm from wreaking revenge on Brian, of course. But that was another story. Brian had had it coming.

It **was** a bit odd, though, thought Norm locking his bike up and heading into the shop. Why **wouldn't** his brothers tell his mum and dad if there was something in it for them? Some way of getting one over on him? Then again, why would his mum and dad suddenly decide to let him buy *Call Of Mortal Combat*? And why **did** Chelsea offer to lend him hers completely out of the blue, **without** any terms and conditions and without any exterior motives, or whatever they were called? There was only one possible explanation, thought Norm. **He** was the only normal one round here. Everyone **else** was flipping weird.

"Can I help you?" said a voice.

"What?" said Norm, still lost in thought.

"Can I help you?"

Norm looked up to see a young woman wearing a Games-R-Us T-shirt, smiling at him. He knew deep down that she **wouldn't** be able to help him. He knew that it was pretty much a lost cause and that there was more chance of fire freezing than there was of him actually getting what he was looking for. But it was worth a shot. Just in case.

"Are you after something in particular, or are you just browsing?"

"Oh, right," said Norm. "Erm, have you got the new *Call Of Mortal Combat*?"

"We certainly have," said the woman setting off. "It's over here."

Norm followed the woman as she made her way to a display, jam-packed full of nothing **but** copies of *Call Of Mortal Combat*.

"For Xbox?"

"Er, yeah, but…"

"Yes?" smiled the Games-R-Us woman.

"Not new ones."

The Games-R-Us woman looked puzzled. "I thought you said the **new** *Call Of Mortal Combat*?"

"Yeah, I did," said Norm. "But not actual **new** ones."

"What, you mean…previously owned copies?"

Norm nodded.

"But…it only came out at midnight on Saturday."

"Yeah, I know," said Norm.

"That's not even forty-eight hours ago."

Gordon flipping Bennet, thought Norm. Just **say** it and put him out of his flipping misery. He already

knew what the answer was. This was just prolonging the agony.

"There ***aren't*** any previously owned copies of *Call Of Mortal Combat* yet."

"Funny you should say that," said a familiar sounding voice.

Norm swivelled around to see his perfect cousin, Danny, grinning from one annoying ear to another. Standing just behind him, was Uncle Steve.

"Hello, Norman."

"Hi, Uncle Steve," said Norm.

"Fancy seeing ***you*** here."

"Yeah. What are the odds?" said Norm.

"That would be almost impossible to calculate," said Danny. "Even for someone as gifted at maths as me."

Norm sighed. Two sentences. That was all it had taken to wind him up. Two flipping sentences.

The Games-R-Us woman smiled at Danny. "You were saying?"

"Yes, I was, wasn't I?" said Danny.

Norm noticed the smile on the Games-R-Us woman's face flicker. It appeared he wasn't the **only** one Danny had managed to instantly irritate.

"Ta da!" said Danny suddenly producing an Xbox game from behind his back.

Norm looked. Sure enough, it was the brand new *Call Of Mortal Combat.*

"But..."

"What?" said Danny. "Why am I getting **rid** of it when I've only just got it?"

"Yeah," said Norm.

"Funny you should say that."

Good, thought Norm. Because right now he could do with a laugh.

"I'm getting the new XStation."

Norm pulled a face. "XStation?"

"Oh, have you not heard of it?" said Danny. "It's **the** new games console. Much better than any other kind."

Norm sighed. And what was he getting **that** for? Going to the toilet? Tidying his room? Finishing his flipping greens?

"You're probably wondering why I'm getting it," said Danny.

"Not really," Norm lied.

"No reason whatsoever," said Danny. "I just am."

Figured, thought Norm.

"So anyway that's why I'm bringing this back. I'm getting rid of **all** my Xbox stuff. Xbox is like, **so** last week."

"I see," said the Games-R-Us woman. "So you're wanting to trade it in?"

"Sure am," said Danny.

"Let's have a look at it, then, shall we?"

"What?" said Danny. "But it's brand new."

"Yes, but I'm afraid I still have to have a look at it. Company policy."

"'Kay," said Danny, somewhat reluctantly handing the game over to the Games-R-Us woman, who proceeded to take the disc out of its box and examine it very carefully.

"Ah."

"What?" said Danny.

"There's a slight scratch."

"Yeah, but…"

"I'm afraid I can only give you five pounds for it."

Danny looked flabbergasted. "Five pounds?"

The Games-R-Us woman nodded.

"I'll give you a tenner for it," said Norm without even thinking about it.

Danny turned his attention to Norm. "What did you just say?"

"I said I'll give you a tenner for it," said Norm.

"Ten pounds?" said Danny.

Norm nodded.

Danny thought for a moment.

"Deal."

"Cool," said Norm getting the twenty pound note out of his back pocket.

"Whoa!" said Uncle Steve holding a hand up. "Not so fast, Norman."

Danny pulled a face. "What, Dad?"

"Just give it to him."

"What?" said Danny.

"You heard," said Uncle Steve.

Danny **had** heard. So had Norm.

"It wasn't actually **your** money in the first place, Danny," said Uncle Steve. "It was me who bought it for you. It was me who queued up at midnight for it. Now give it to your cousin. For **nothing!**"

"But..." began Danny.

"Just do as I say," said Uncle Steve.

"I raised the most money for destitute donkeys, remember?"

"Yes," said Uncle Steve. "And I'm buying you a brand new XStation for no reason whatsoever. **Remember?**"

Norm **tried** not to smirk as Danny handed the game over, but it was difficult not to. Not that he particularly cared whether **Danny** saw him smirking or not. But it was probably best that Uncle Steve didn't notice.

"You don't **mind**, do you, Norman?" said Uncle Steve.

"What?" said Norm. "I mean, pardon?"

"You don't **mind** getting Danny's old copy?"

"Er, no, not at all," said Norm. Which was something of an understatement. Not only did Norm **not** mind, he was secretly wanting to burst into song, jump up and down and turn flipping cartwheels. Not that Norm could actually turn cartwheels. But that wasn't the point. The point **was**, he was so happy he could have **kissed** Uncle Steve.

"Good."

"Uncle Steve?"

"Yes, Norman?"

"Thanks," said Norm.

"You're very welcome," said Uncle Steve. "Isn't he, Danny?"

But Danny didn't say anything. He had a face like thunder.

"I said **isn't** he, Danny?"

"Whatever," mumbled Danny.

"You know I can actually sort that scratch out for you, if you want?" said the Games-R-Us woman, to Norm.

"Really?" said Norm.

"We've got a special machine. It'll cost you a fiver, though."

A fiver? thought Norm. For a less than two day old copy of the brand new *Call Of Mortal Combat*?

"Well?" said the Games-R-Us woman. "What do you say?"

Norm burst into a huge, doughnut-eating grin.

"I say that's an abso-flipping-lute bargain!"

CHAPTER 20

As Norm opened the front door, he was greeted by a warm blast of cooking fumes from the direction of the kitchen.

Mmmm, de-flipping-licious, thought Norm taking a deep breath. The unmistakeable whiff of chips. One of his all-time *favourite* smells. Even supermarket own-brand oven chips, which these chips undoubtedly were. He really didn't care. He really didn't care what he ate *with* them either. Supermarket own-brand burgers? Supermarket own-brand bangers?

Supermarket own-brand pretty much anything basically. It simply didn't matter to Norm. Because whatever it was would be a billion times better than carrot and flipping lemon grass cutting soup or whatever **other** freakish food it was that his perfect cousins would be tucking into round about now. If they weren't too busy preventing global warming, or saving flipping flatulent flamingos from extinction, or whatever.

Norm finally exhaled and smiled to himself. It was good to be back in this stupid little house. And it wasn't every day he could say **that**.

Even better, Norm had the almost-brand spanking new *Call Of Mortal Combat* in his hands – **and** fifteen quid in his back pocket. Things, thought Norm, were **definitely** looking up. And it wasn't every day he could say **that** either!

"What's that?" said Dave appearing at the foot of the stairs.

"What's **what?**"
said Norm looking
round.

"That," said Dave with
a nod of his head.

Norm sighed. "What do
you **think** it is, Dave?"

"An Xbox game."

"Well, then. Why flipping ask?"

"Yeah, but **which** Xbox game?"

"What's it to you?" said Norm.

"What's it to you?" Dave shot back.

"Uh?" said Norm. "That doesn't even make **sense**."

"Yeah, it does."

Gordon flipping Bennet, thought Norm. Dave wasn't only **shrewd**. He could also be incredibly argumentative. **And** stubborn.

"If you must know, it's *Call Of Mortal Combat*."

"Whoa. The **new** one?"

Norm nodded.

"Coooooooool!" said Dave.

"Boys?" called Norm's mum. "It's tea time!"

"Coming, Mum!" yelled Dave.

They looked at each other for a moment.

"Well?" said Dave.

"What?" said Norm.

"Have you got something to say to me?"

Norm shrugged. "Dunno. Have I?"

"I saved your...you know?"

"My what?" said Norm.

"Your you-know-what," said Dave.

"No, I don't actually," said Norm. "My what?"

"Your bottom," whispered Dave.

"You saved my **bottom?**" said Norm.

"I could've told."

"Told **what?**"

"About how come Brian's jumper ended up shrinking."

Sssssh!" said Norm, finally figuring out what Dave

was on about and looking
round to make sure they
weren't being overheard.

"Well?" said Dave.

Norm thought for a
moment.

"Thanks?"

"**Thanks?**" said Dave.
"Is that it?"

Norm pulled a face. "Yeah."

"I thought you might have been..."

"What?"

"A bit more...grateful?" said Dave.

And what was **that** supposed to mean? thought
Norm. It was beginning to look like Dave knowing
about Norm's cunning plan **might** just turn out to
be a problem after all.

"Boys?" called Norm's mum from the kitchen.

"Coming, Mum!" called Dave.

But Dave showed no sign of going anywhere and stayed exactly where he was, as if he was waiting for Norm to make the next move.

Norm did a quick mental calculation. He'd been given twenty pounds to buy *Call Of Mortal Combat*. He'd ended up getting it for free. OK, so he'd paid a fiver to get the scratch removed. But that still left fifteen quid to spend on whatever he wanted to spend it on.

"Five pounds," said Norm.

"What?" said Dave.

"Five pounds to stay schtum."

"Stay what?" said Dave.

"To keep your trap shut."

Dave thought for a moment.

"Deal."

"Excellent," said Norm. "And then no more nonsense."

"What do you mean, no more nonsense?" said Dave.

"I mean that's it," said Norm. "No more bribery. No more blackmail. End of."

They looked at each other.

"Fair enough?" said Norm.

Dave nodded. "Fair enough."

"Come on, then," said Norm, heading into the

kitchen, where Brian and his mum were already seated at the table.

"Where's, Dad?" said Dave, following.

"Right here," said Norm's dad appearing in the doorway.

"Where have you been?" said Norm's mum.

"On the phone," said Norm's dad.

"Really?" said Norm's mum. "Who to?"

"Your brother."

"Steven?"

What? thought Norm. Uncle Steve? Surely not? Not *already*. Oh well. It was nice while it lasted.

"You'll never guess what happened," said Norm's dad.

"No, what?" said Norm's mum.

"Danny *gave* Norman a copy of *Call Of Mortal Combat*!"

"Gave?" said Norm's mum.

"Gave," said Norm's dad.

"For free?"

Norm's dad nodded. "For free!"

"Amazing!" said Norm's mum.

"I know!" said Norm. "I was just about to tell you."

Norm's mum looked at Norm for a moment.

"Really?"

"What?" said Norm in mock outrage. "Well, of *course* I was, Mum! What do you take me for?"

Norm's mum smiled. "Sorry, love. I know you were."

"Give it to me, then," said Norm's dad.

"What?" said Norm. "The money?"

"No, love," said Norm's mum. "You give **me** the money."

"You give **me** the game," said Norm's dad, holding his hand out expectantly.

"But…"

"But what, Norman?"

"Why?"

"Why?" said Norm's dad.

Norm nodded.

"Because you're still banned from the Xbox, that's why."

Gordon flipping Bennet, thought Norm. He just **_knew_** it was too flipping good to be true.

"Ha, ha," said Brian.

"Shut up, Brian, you little freak," hissed Norm.

Want more Norm? Then you'll love this flipping brilliant Norm-themed activity book!

Packed with loads of great Norm facts, pant-wettingly-hilarious jokes and crazy doodle activities!

OUT NOW!

Norm's Vital Statistics

Age: Nearly 13

Height: 1.53 metres

Eyes: Two

Likes: Bikes

Doesn't like: Chelsea

Favourite word: Abso-flipping-lutely

Least favourite word: Hormones

Thinks: Everything's unfair

Draw a picture of Norm here:

Just Flipping Say It

Fill in the bubbles with questions, statements or anything else you feel like saying.

'Aw, Man!'

Being forced to visit his perfect cousins at the weekend makes Norm go:

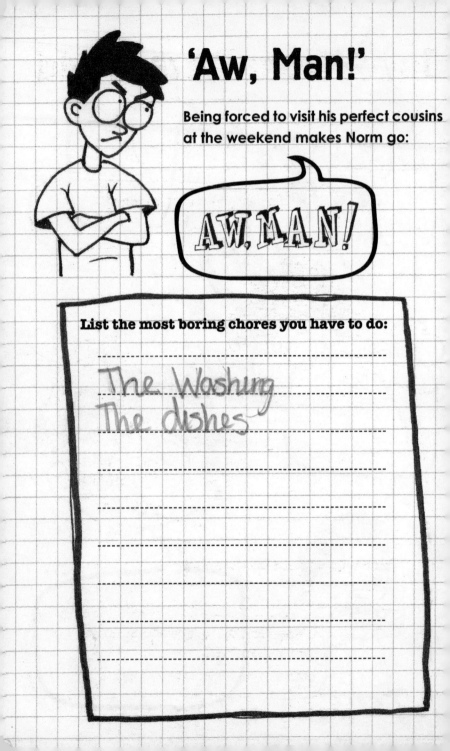

AW, MAN!

List the most boring chores you have to do:

The Washing
The dishes

Jokes from Pizza World

Which is the left side of a pizza?
The side that hasn't been eaten.

'Waiter, will my pizza be long?'
'No sir, it will be round.'

Which type of pizza do dogs like?
Puparoni.

What was Good King Wenceslas's favourite pizza?
Deep pan, crisp and even.

THE WORLD OF NORM

MAY CONTAIN PRIZES

WANT TO WIN SOME WORLD OF NORM GOODIES?

ABSO-FLIPPING-LUTELY

WELL CHECK OUT THE WORLD OF NORM WEBSITE AND ENTER THE COMPETITION ONLINE!

www.worldofnorm.co.uk